Spunky Mellie Wheaton, recovering from a case of terminally bad judgment when it comes to men, is determined to concentrate on her new job in Hawaii as a marine biologist. That is, until her fishing line tangles with handsome hunk TJ, lead singer in the boy band *TJ and the Sharks* at her brother's wedding. Dismissing him as simply another hot surfer dude who sings, she sees he has his sights set on her.

TJ is more than meets the eye. He's an up and coming expert in oceanic ecology and heads a prestigious research study Mellie joins. While serious about sharks— especially tiger sharks— he finds himself nibbling a fish here and there but has yet to land the catch of his dreams. Soon he's entangled in Mellie's line and becomes hooked by her charms, but Mellie isn't that easily captured.

Time spent together on the ocean conducting research under the balmy trade winds and hot Hawaiian sunshine lures them toward love until Wolfe, her ex, follows her to Oahu determined to capture and land her heart once and for all. It's all up to Mellie. Can she survive her tsunami of feelings? Keep her independence? Or will one of the men become her catch of the day?

Promises on the Beach
Copyright © 2020 Kathy Kalmar
ISBN: 978-1-4874-2949-2
Cover art by Martine Jardin

Published by eXtasy Books Inc or
Devine Destinies, an imprint of eXtasy Books Inc

Look for us online at:
www.eXtasybooks.com or www.devinedestinies.com

PROMISES ON THE BEACH

BY

KATHY KALMAR

DEDICATION

To Larry, who gave me my very own second chance to love, more happiness than I could have believed possible, and healed three broken hearts in the process.
and
Terry Wilson, songwriter, who is the prototype for TJ Matthews.

In Memoriam

To my forever friend, Linda Wilson, whose skills, talents, and belief in me and my work led to this publication. Ours was a relationship forged in the fires of pain, loss, love and laughter.

Acknowledgment

For Carolyn Gilbreath, her counsel and encouragement made this a better book. She is my Best Friend Forever and Beta reader extraordinaire. And to Doug Marple, webmaster, who keeps the social media site wheels turning. I'm grateful to you all. Dr. Ken Howard for his shark expertise.

And with great gratitude, I acknowledge Jay Austin, extraordinary Editor in Chief, maker of dreams come true; Debbie Nygaard, excellent editor; Brigit Vries, Assistant to the Editor in Chief for everything she does to get things just right: Martine Jardin, artist; R.C. Matthews and The Greater Detroit Romance Writers of America; and you, my loyal readers.

Disclaimer

Any information regarding sharks that is incorrect is mine and mine alone.

PROLOGUE

Dean Chance Matthew's desk phone rang. He pressed *talk.* "Zach is on line three," his secretary's voice announced.

He immediately picked up the receiver, and Zach started babbling before he even said *hello.*

"She's what?" Chance screeched. "Your mother isn't due yet."

"Sounds to me like she needs to go to the hospital," Zach, his thirteen-year-old stepson said.

Chance blew out a breath. *In-out-in-out. Just like the birth classes taught us.*

"It's three weeks too early!" He ran his hand through his slightly long hair. With the babies coming, he just hadn't had time to get a trim. If things had gone according to plan, he'd have kept his hair appointment. But the surprise baby shower had put the kibosh to that.

He was still dealing with the haul from the baby shower held the previous day. There was a ton of stuff to up pack, assemble, and put in place.

Caren can't be in labor now! His breathing was fast and shallow. He began to perspire. He wiped a hand across his sweaty forehead and noticed his hand was shaking. He inhaled, but letting the air out again was not as easy as actually doing it.

Calm down. Women have babies every day. But the woman having a baby this time wasn't just any woman. It was Caren, his love, his life, and she was having his baby — early! *Snap out of it. Pay attention!*

Zach was talking. "I know, but Mom said to call you, cuz

1

it's happening now. Hurry up and get home."

"Okay. I'll be right there." He snatched his keys off the desk and barreled out the door, the receiver still in his grip. He pulled the phone off the desk in his hurry. It hit the floor with a bounce and disconnected. *Shit!* "My phone! Where the hell is my damn phone?"

His secretary, hearing the commotion, rushed into his office, grabbed his cell phone, handed it to him, and said in a dry tone, "In your hand now. Settle down. Babies are born every day. "

"My babies aren't!" Chance glanced at the cell phone and grinned. "Call my sister-in-law, Nikki Nolan. You have her number. Tell her to call Grandpa Gus, and Grandma Daisy, too."

"Done and done. They're all on their way over. Settle down. Drive safely."

Heart in his stomach, Chance Matthews sped home to his pregnant wife. *Let them be okay.* His first wife, Angie, and the baby she carried had died in a car accident. He could not lose Caren. *Not after all we've been through. Hell, we've been through enough.*

Chance had been ready to give up when Angie had died at the hands of a drunk driver. He had gone a little crazy then. It had been a daily struggle to keep going. For years afterward, he'd led a half-life. But he'd found a reason to live again after he met Caren on a Hawaiian vacation they had both won.

Caren had nearly drowned on that trip, getting caught by a rogue riptide. And if that wasn't enough, an erupting volcano had threatened Chance's life. They needed to catch a break. Chance only hoped God saw it his way. *Please!*

He pulled into their driveway as Nikki, Caren's sister, was getting out of her car.

Their adoptive grandparents, Gus and Daisy, were calming Emily, his stepdaughter, standing on the porch.

Caren stood next to them, gritting her teeth and holding her abdomen, obviously struggling to bite back screams as the pain doubled her over. Low groans escaped through her clenched lips.

"Take her and go," Gus said grimly. "Daisy and I have the kids, they'll be fine. Get out of here!"

Caren's pregnancy had been normal. Until this. She was approaching her mid-thirties, but she wasn't technically a high-risk pregnancy. *If I lose her now . . . and the baby . . .*

His wife struggled to give him a smile, but it came across more like a grimace.

Chance helped buckle her into the car while Nikki got into the back seat. Then he sped off, barely registering the stop sign as he barreled right through it. He took the next corner on two wheels and barely noticed the red light. Then, at last, he skidded to a stop in front of the emergency room entrance.

"I'm fine," Caren said. "Relax. Breathe. I gave birth early with both Zach and Emily."

"Are you trying to reassure me or you?"

"Both." She grinned.

The security attendant helped Caren into the nearby wheelchair while Chance dealt with the paperwork.

Mark Wheaton, his soon to be brother-in-law, met Chance on the maternity floor.

"Nikki joined Caren in the labor room," he told Mark, gesturing down the hallway. Chance again raked his hands through his hair as he paced the confines of the hall. A nurse finally showed up to take him to the labor room.

Someone was yelling at the top of her lungs. "Drugs! Give me drugs no matter what my birth plan says."

Chance winced and glanced at Mark. "Caren has a set of lungs on her." He would recognize her voice anywhere.

She had warned him she might cave in to the pain.

He wasn't allowed to let her give in. Those were his marching orders.

Nikki was not under those orders, so she dashed out of the room and went off to find someone who could help. She had been with Caren for the births of both Zach and Emily.

Caren had gone without drugs the first two times, but she was seven years older now.

Chance threw up his hands. *Should I talk her off the ledge?*

No one argued with her, but by the time Nikki found someone, the first baby had crowned. Drugs weren't an option any longer. They transferred Caren to the delivery room.

Chance accompanied her, stroking her arm, trying to support her.

Nikki followed shortly after she donned the hospital garb. She straightened her hair cover and appeared fully prepared to encourage and support both Chance and Caren.

"I have to push," Caren yelled.

Minutes later, at three-thirty-three in the afternoon, his newborn daughter quickly abandoned the birth canal and nearly flew into Chance's arms.

He sat there stunned. *Don't fumble the ball, Matthews.*

Calla Matthews had arrived in record time — less than four hours from first pain until the birth.

Two minutes later, Lily Matthews emerged crying lustily.

Caren, Chance, Calla, and Lily were all crying.

Oh my God, I'm a Dad!

Caren choked out, "Can you believe after all that angst about having a baby or not, we end up with twins?" She fell back on the delivery table looking wiped out, utterly spent. "Who'd believe it?"

"Hey, after all that's gone on, none of us has any business being surprised," Nikki answered.

The babies cried because it was what newborns did to use their new set of lungs and keep breathing, but the doctor pronounced them healthy and whole.

Nikki looked at Mark. She wasn't smiling, but she wasn't mad. "There's something I need to tell you before we go any further."

"That's a classic *We need to talk* if I ever heard one," her new fiancé replied. "Should I be worried? We already had our first fight."

"And make-up sex," Nikki noted. "No, but it's nothing that simple. I have a son."

"Say what?"

"Well, I *will* have a son," Nikki started to explain.

"Are you psychic? We haven't discussed children much. I know you could be pregnant after all, but how do you know it's a boy?"

"Because I adopted him. It's final, and I'll take custody soon after we get home."

"And you didn't tell me, why?"

"Because I never expected your proposal, for one thing," she said.

"And?"

"I didn't expect my answer to be *yes* either," Nikki said with a grin, taking the chance to kiss his lips.

Nikki had set the wheels for the adoption in motion over a year earlier. Even though she was adopting ten-year-old Benjamin, she hadn't counted on getting an email from Lindsey, the adoption caseworker from St. Jacques, *now* either. They had told her it could take well over a year, but everything happened suddenly. For sure, she hadn't planned on being Caren's wedding planner. She certainly could not have foreseen Mark Wheaton and his role in her life. She definitely hadn't planned to fall in love with Mark either, but she had.

Nikki was a no-nonsense reality therapist with her own practice. Usually, her life proceeded along certain practical and well thought out lines. Lately, though, things were going widely off the prescribed path. She was thirty-seven-years-old and — at the time — had no prospects for marriage, but that didn't mean she couldn't have a child and family of her own. Hence her decision to adopt Benjamin. She could always break off an engagement made in haste, but she could not, would not sacrifice this adoption. She hoped Mark was cool with it. If not, her engagement would be the shortest one on record.

Mark smiled at her and shrugged his shoulders. "Cool. I'm going to be a dad!"

CHAPTER ONE: ONCE UPON A TIME

TJ Morgan was getting set to windsurf off Kailua beach. He had just returned from another gig, a wedding, and a hot chick, Mellie was there. It was hard to focus on assembling his rig when visions of Mellie occupied his head. *Did she have to look like Kate Upton? Wasn't it enough that she was pretty with legs up to her tight ass? But the hair. Really? And world-class cleavage too!*

The winds kicked up, TJ maneuvered the jib line, and the sail caught the trade winds. The weather was perfect for kite surfing. Then nature did its thing and carried him away with the tide. He rode with thoughts of Mellie in his head and the wind in his sail. He always imagined life couldn't get any better than the rush he got from soaring across the surf. It was a high unlike any other until he met Mellie.

Now that he had, he found she was just as exhilarating. Previously, he had sworn by windsurfing. But was it *mo bettah,* as his friend, a tour guide named Kekoa, had always insisted? Thoughts of Mellie caused a real high like he'd never experienced before.

He must have been caught up in his vision of her, because he suddenly noticed he was getting hot. He eased one leg off the board, holding tightly to the boom as he carefully moved his other leg off the board, performing a body drag to cool off.

The body drag didn't work, however, because now he was thinking that maybe tandem windsurfing would be something worth experiencing. Thinking of Mellie's body pressed close to his as they sped across the water made him hot all over again.

Mellie Wheaton pulled her motor scooter into the University of Hawaii Honolulu's student parking lot. She was dressed like any other student in Hawaii, wearing shorts and a *UH* t-shirt. She was a senior transferring from the University of Michigan, majoring in marine biology and specializing in tiger sharks. Transferring here had been well worth it. Tiger sharks frequented the local waters.

Although she had gone to the Atlantic Ocean for much of her lab work, she needed Pacific Ocean experience for more than one reason. There was a *shark* back home in Michigan, and she needed to escape him.

Her brother, Mark Wheaton, owned a condo on Oahu, where she would reside, cutting costs of an apartment or dorm. Since Mark was helping her with tuition, the arrangement worked well for them both.

Mark had barked some about her losing some lab credits. While he was at it, he harped on her poor judgment concerning her choices in men, but eventually, he chalked it up to her youth. It was Mark's typical response.

Rich was my high school bad boy crush. A girl can be expected to fall for a bad boy at least once in her life, can't she? Seriously? Besides, twenty-two is not all that young.

Mark was in his thirties and paying her way, so she wasn't going to argue. At times like these, she wished she could distract him from his *boring* lecture. Yada, yada. But alas, distraction wasn't going to happen.

"Where do you stand with the University? What's left? Do you have a plan?"

Mellie smirked.

Mark slapped his forehead. "Of course, you do. Why do I even bother to ask?"

All Mellie's basic coursework for the degree was completed. Although she was a senior in class ranking, she was low in seniority when it came to field and lab work in Hawaii. So far, her work on Lake Michigan and the Atlantic had given her a rich and varied background. Still, she had to do the grunt work in the field in the Pacific.

She had some marine biology courses that took place in the lecture hall, but today she was scheduled to go out on the *Meyers Research* boat in the afternoon. She secured her helmet to her scooter, put on her sun-visor, and hiked to the Science Building for class, slinging her backpack and lap-top over her shoulders. Although she wasn't dressed up nor in a swimsuit, she noticed she got her fair share of male attention as she strode across the campus.

Once in class, she took avid notes throughout the two-hour session. The professor displayed podcasts of his research using the smartboard. She was glad a great deal of her coursework used video because, it was much more engaging than the texts or straight lectures. As a rule, she paid attention to PowerPoint, but lectures not so much.

As class ended, she decided to eat her lunch ocean side at the launch site for the Hawaii Institute of Marine Biology, HIMB. It was a thirty-minute ride to the site.

Done windsurfing, TJ began to prepare for the research he was doing for the day. But his thoughts roamed when he started thinking of Mellie again. He was glad he had worked up the nerve to talk to her. *Thank heaven I did. What a woman. Hot, hot, hot, that's what she is.*

From their conversation, he had discovered Mellie was Mark Wheaton's kid sister. Mark owned World Travel & Tour and was responsible for him meeting Mellie. *Where did I get the idea to put a tape on, ending the set to go talk to her? Was it fate? God? A stroke of uncommon good luck? Whatever.*

He had stepped way outside of character that day.

He was still recuperating from his failed relationship with Nina, but he found himself approaching a beautiful woman, a stranger, saying, "Hi, I'm TJ Morgan, wedding singer extraordinaire" — *where the hell did that come from?* — "and you're . . ."

The woman cocked an eye at him and responded, "I'm Michelle Melody Wheaton. My friends call me Mellie."

She paused just then when *I Only Have Eyes For You* began to play.

Whatever possessed him to add that cut to the tape, he couldn't say, but he was glad he had because, in a clear, full voice, Mellie began to sing along with it. *She's surprisingly good.* He found himself growing, if possible, even more excited than he already was.

"Hey, you can sing."

"Obviously." Then she laughed as she added, "With a name like Melody, you almost have to sing, dontcha think?"

What TJ thought was that she was as beautiful as a Hawaiian sunset, all peachy and golden. "No, I mean it. You're really good." He was being straight up sincere with no bullshit designed to flatter or impress her.

"So are you," she returned. "Obviously."

She continued singing along when he quipped, "I could call you by your initial, M.M." He winked.

"You make me sound like that old soup jingle. You know the really, really old one. She sang it.

"Should we see if that's true?"

She nodded consenting.

Then he bent his head and kissed her. Running his tongue over his lips, tasting her, he gave a lopsided grin and announced, "Good, very good." *Delicious!*

The tape was ending, and his bandmates were getting

ready to play a second set. "Sorry, I have to get back and sing for my supper. I sure hope to see you around. Where do you hang out?"

"The beach," she said, flushed from his kiss, he hoped.

TJ Morgan was many things. One was a musician with a band, *the Sharks,* that played at *The Hatcheck Lounge.* He wrote music and lyrics, too. He was also an all-around smart fellow who had his future all charted.

True, something was missing, but he wasn't that concerned. He'd find the missing link sooner or later. He never made promises that he could not keep. He'd learned that at his grandmother's knee. *Gram, I keep my word, and I always will, just as I promised I would.* At the time, he and Gram were sitting on the porch swing back at the farm in Illinois.

"Never make a promise you don't keep or plan to keep. Show me your pinky finger." She extended hers, kinking it through his, and shook both. "See how it's done? This means it can *never* be broken. We're linked — pinky promise."

TJ arrived at HIMB for his afternoon excursion and spotted the woman that had occupied his thought all morning. Although Mellie obviously hadn't seen him, he couldn't take his eyes off her as she applied sunscreen liberally over long legs just beginning to tan.

TJ was a doctoral graduate student specializing in all things shark. He was headed out again to investigate a shark incident off Maui when he saw her.

Mellie appeared absorbed in what she was doing and was joining a group of apparent newbies as they lugged equipment to the boat. *Wonder what her focus is? Mine is shark attacks and windsurfing. And, oh yeah, music. But now it seems it's a laser beam on one beautiful Mellie Wheaton.* With an effort, TJ switched his attention to his task.

It took his full concentration, but he eventually pulled his

11

thoughts from Mellie and put them on the launch they would use to sail the three hours to Maui's coastline. The shark incident was not fatal, but a surfer had been hurt. Generally, shark *attacks* were rare.

Sharks roamed the ocean convinced they were predators, not prey. It seemed almost like that gave them a sort of confidence. TJ knew he had to be careful with his line of thought. Sharks were animals, not thinking nor acting like humans, but sometimes their behavior made him wonder about that. *Once tasting human flesh, did they want more?*

Normally sharks were not aggressive. Being at the top of the food chain, there was no need for aggression. But *something* had occurred off Maui, and he was with a team charged with the responsibility of finding out what happened and why. Sharks were almost always in cruise mode *except* when hunting for prey. Usually, the prey wasn't of the human form. *What gives with this recent turn of events?*

Several things *could* account for the incident. Mistaking a surfer for prey, nearby fishing, or some other lure. *Hell, it could just be hunger. A nice tasty dolphin or a sea turtle he was after and missed. Who knows?* TJ planned to find out.

The sea and sharks captured his attention. He could hardly wait to leave, but there were other duties he needed to complete before the launch. The team was awaiting the call to action.

Mellie boarded the boat and was soon engaged in baiting hooks for the study the outing demanded. *Eww. This is one smelly job I thought I was through with. Not fun being the newbie.* She wrinkled her brow and nose as she did the job, hoping to earn the respect of the senior field crew. She hauled equipment, untangled lines, baited hooks, and did everything she could to gain skill, know-how, and experience. After another successful routine jaunt, they returned to shore.

She gathered her things, retrieved her motor scooter, and headed to the condo. She spent the next several weeks doing the same thing. The *rinse and repeat* tasks were tedious, but she enjoyed it all the same.

As usual, she was reviewing her day when thoughts of Wolfe, her last disastrous love, crept into her mind. *If only he'd been what he appeared to be . . . If this is love, it's sure not what it's cracked up to be. Still, I want him. When will this yearning go away? What is it about men? What do they want? How could Wolfe be such a . . . such a wolf? Why did he cheat on me? What did I do wrong? Sleep with him too soon? Not enough? What?*

Thoughts like these got her nowhere. *Should I see a therapist? Wouldn't Mark love that? Wait, he's engaged to a therapist. Nikki. Hmm . . . what if I emailed her?*

CHAPTER TWO: CHATTER

M ellie felt comfortable reaching out to Nikki, especially since they were almost sisters-in-law. She decided to lay everything on the line.

To: Nikki
From: Mellie Wheaton
Subject: Advice
Hi Nikki,
I know we started off on the wrong foot. Walking in on you and Mark, uh, bonding. Literally! Who knew? Talk about shocking! For all of us! Who knew that you and Mark were a thing? Truly, I am so sorry for intruding. How maddening and upsetting for both of you. And it was pretty embarrassing for me, too. And worse when you thought I was one of Mark's conquests-yikes! And you thinking I was Mark's **girlfriend** *instead of his* **sister***, holy moly. All that being what it is, after all we have been through, and with you being a therapist who's practically family now that you two are en-gaged . . . What I'm trying to ask is, do you think I need therapy? I hope you don't mind me asking. I don't know whether Mark told you about Wolfe or not, but we broke up. That's one reason I left Michigan early. Breaking up hurts like hell. I don't know if it's my pride or my heart, but I'm feeling, like, confused. When will this pain end? This obsessing about Wolfe? He's all I think about. I know there's a six-hour time difference, so email whenever you can. Hugs, Mellie*

There. Maybe Nikki will have some answers. Mellie pulled a frozen healthy meal from the freezer and nuked it. She carried it out to the lanai. *Lanai sounds so much better than balcony. Romantic. Ugh, don't want to think about romance shit.*

Mellie sat at the small table overlooking the Pacific Ocean. The sky was stained mauve from the setting sun, and Diamond Head shadowed the water, making it appear inky blue. She ate, enjoying both the view and the food, but not her thoughts. Even meditating when she was through eating didn't calm her turmoil. No matter how hard she tried to clear her mind, she found herself thinking of Wolfe again.

It was true, Wolfe wanted to get her back. While he had tried to contact her by cell and email, she knew she could . . . Never. Ever. Trust. Him. Again. *Jeez! I sound like a sick version of Taylor Swift. Will I ever feel normal again?* She didn't take his calls, and she blocked him on her Facebook page. *Some friend! Cheater.* She wanted to be over him and free of the nagging feelings he had left behind in his wake. Wolfe was so worldly and experienced. So wise. *Hmph, if he's so wise, why did he sleep with Monique? She's such a slut.*

Nonetheless, Mellie still ached for him. He was her senior by ten years, and she had been charmed by his position in life. He seemed so debonair and strong.

She loved his sense of style. He took care with his wardrobe. It contrasted sharply with the guys her age, who seemed addicted to grunge and facial stubble. Few men could carry that look off well. Not even Brad Pitt.

That reminded her of the wedding singer, *TJ, who looked a lot like Brad Pitt with his sun- streaked blond hair, firm body, tanned, yum.*

She smiled as she recalled bantering and singing with him. Then she mentally gave herself a slap in the forehead for *those* thoughts. She was done with men, *all* men, even men who looked as strikingly good as TJ. *Focus. Think of school, not men. What I need is a job, girlfriend.*

But no matter what she did, her thoughts continued revolving around Wolfe, as if her mind were an endless tape, always looping back to Wolfe. She had thought Wolfe was her type. He had gone so far as to give her a key to his apartment. *That had to mean something, right? He said I love you as well.*

He was so intelligent. Half the time, he lived in his head. *Apparently, both heads, his penis included. Oh, Wolfe.* He dazzled her with his sophistication, yet he still had a boyish charm about him. He turned her on like a hot water faucet. *Sleeping not only with someone else, not just anyone, but with Monique. Buzzkill.*

Monique was an old rival from high school. She'd also gone so far as pledging for the same sorority that Mellie had. When Mellie found out, she withdrew from the pledge process. She had had enough of Monique in high school. But no matter how she tried to avoid the woman, Monique Montáge still tried to insert herself into Mellie's life. So much so, Mellie had caught Monique and Wolfe *in the act* on the sectional in Wolfe's apartment. Once she saw them, that was that.

Without further ado, Mellie had turned on her heel, marched into his bedroom, threw her few things she kept there into her duffle bag and walked out of his life. *And apparently out of his heart.* While he did try to explain by blaming it all on Monique and an early mid-life crisis, Mellie was having none of it.

She had finished up her summer classes, and once exams were over, she flew to Oahu to her brother. *And look how that turned out. How was I supposed to know he was banging Nikki in his hotel suite? The desk attendant gave me a keycard. My bad. If Mark had just given me a key to his condo . . . but nooo. Well, then I wouldn't have interrupted them, now would I? Oops!*

Her thoughts raced on. *Once Mark got over the shock of my rude interruption, even he agreed I made a smart move, leaving Michigan early. Mark's surprisingly understanding. He thinks a physical separation from Wolfe is a solid strategy, since I was transferring to the University of Hawaii anyway.*

Mellie giggled, recalling how irritated Mark had been

about Nikki thinking *Mellie* was his *lover. What a hoot.*

She knew Mark had struggled with getting over his anger and pride about that misunderstanding. But once he had, he stood solidly behind and beside Mellie and her Wolfe problem.

She remembered telling Mark, "But he said he loved me. How could he sleep with someone else? He said we were exclusive. Or at least, I thought we were. But then he adds insult to injury by sleeping with Monique."

"Forget about 'em." Mark had said. "She's a skank, and he's a dick." And that was how he saw it.

Nothing was going to change Mark's opinion of Wolfe. Not that Mellie wanted him to, but after Rich and *that* experience, she knew Mark was questioning, if not her taste in men, at least her judgment concerning them. *Okay, so I probably was infatuated or in lust with Rich. He was such a handsome badass boy! Who wouldn't jump in the sack with him? S'right, falling in love was a mistake, but what the hell, I am only human after all. I was just a high school kid.*

More than once, Mark had said, "Wolfe gives men a bad name. You were a sitting duck. He preys on women, the younger, the better."

Mellie sighed. She knew he was right, but it still smarted. Like she'd written Nikki, it hurt like hell. She went back inside the condo, typed up her lab report, emailed it, read her textbook, then sank into a warm bubble bath.

She loved the sensation of the hot bath-oiled, silky water on her skin, but it reminded her of Wolfe's touch. He was a good lover after all was said and done. That was probably what still had her hooked.

Should have taken a cold shower instead. She wrapped herself in one of the sumptuous fluffy bath sheets Mark had stocked the place with, donned a *UH* jersey, and went to bed.

Despite her resolutions not to think of men, she dreamed of TJ and the kiss they had shared.

When she awoke the next morning, she ate some pineapple and a bagel and checked her email. She was happy to see a reply from Nikki.

To: Mellie Wheaton
From: Nikki
Subject: Re: Advice
You can email me or call anytime. Maybe not now since there is that six-hour time difference, lol. Seriously, I'm willing to listen. I say what I mean, and sometimes it's not pretty. You up for that? So far, the most I can tell you is your feelings are justified. It's normal to feel hurt, rejected, even depressed. I sense, though, that there's a tad bit more there regarding Wolfe. How did you two meet? Until I know you are okay with my frankness, I'll wait before I say anything more. While I think everyone benefits from therapy, I don't know if you need it. I'll refer you to someone I know if you wish. Mark and I don't discuss you. We're busy with some things in our lives – like wedding plans. Take care. Nikki.

To: Nikki
From: Mellie Wheaton
Subject: Re: Re: Advice
Thanks for your quick reply. It's nice to know I'm normal. I took classes with Wolfe, who was my prof and advisor. Before you go nuts, I didn't date him until he was no longer my professor. I'm up for whatever you have to say. I'll put my big girl *panties on. I can take it. Hugs, Mellie*

To: Mellie Wheaton
From: Nikki
Subject: Concerns
Part of what you may be feeling is embarrassment. Older man, professor, seduces young female student. Seriously, this smack of harassment, and it may be an issue for campus security. It should

be reported. Hugs, Nik.

To: Nikki
From: Mellie Wheaton
Subject: Re: Concerns
Hi Nikki, That seems a little extreme. He didn't seduce me. I was dating *him. We fell for each other. It was mutual. I reached the age of consent years ago. Besides, I'm not even a student there anymore, so it's a non-issue.*

To: Mellie Wheaton
From: Nikki
Subject: More Concerns
Because he was in a position of power over you by age and profession, it is *an issue. He's likely to do it to someone else. My sister's a professor there. We can ask her about the ethics of this and the reporting process if you like. I strongly advise you to report it. Think of it as part of your healing process. You should feel better about yourself once you see that you can stop him from exploiting other students. Told you, I keep it real. Like Dr. Phil, I tell it as it is. Hugs, Nikki*

Hmm . . .

Mellie checked her email for other messages before she left — just in case. She had an early morning lab. *I wonder what we'll be doing today. Good thing I checked. We're working out at the HIMB. That's on Coconut Island. What's up with that?* She grabbed her backpack, sprayed on sunblock, pulled her ponytail through the back of her baseball cap, and headed the door.

CHAPTER THREE: RESEARCH

TJ headed to HIMB to meet up with his crew. He and his research partners needed to go back to Maui to see what more they could learn from the recent shark incidents. There had been five incidents, and counting . . . The other day, they had retrieved parts of the surfboard and some evidence of fishing. This time he needed a larger crew and more lab students.

Earlier, he had put in a request for a consistent crew, and not just the standard fieldwork rotation of newbies. He had talked to Dr. Rolland, who agreed with the idea, since the shark incidents were increasing in frequency. A regular crew would help. The crew was scheduled to meet at dawn since the trip would take three hours.

Arriving at HIMB, he was glad to see Burt Raines-Forest and Deb Rivers, his research partners. He had asked Deb to select seasoned field students who had the experience and expertise for this part of the work. There was a time for rookies, but this wasn't one of them. He didn't have the usual patience for them now. Already there'd been twice as many shark encounters as last year — most off Maui's Makena shoreline.

Deb was headed over to a group of students assembled under the palm trees, which were flocked by tropical, flowering bushes and ferns. When he looked closer, he could not believe his eyes. Lo and behold, one of the lab students was none other than Mellie Wheaton. *Well, hellooo. Oh, baby! Who knew she was into marine biology?* There was a lot he wanted to get into with her. He gave her a huge welcoming smile with a wink.

Mellie gaped at TJ as he approached the group. She knew he was in a band and that he surfed, but what was he doing here? Mark had filled her in a little at Caren and Chance's wedding reception when surfing came up as part of the conversation. *I thought he was a surfer dude.*

Her attention shifted as Deb said, "TJ, Burt, and I are the research crew you'll be working with. TJ is chief researcher."

Mellie hoped her surprise didn't show on her face. *Research crew — WTF? There's more to him than meets the eye.*

"And chief bottle washer, too," he said and grinned.

The group chuckled, acknowledging the pecking order.

Mellie smiled her greeting, and said, "No more bottle washing for you. I understand that's the newbie's job. That means, I wash the bottles from here on out."

"I guess that means I'll help," Sandy said. "I'm a lab rat, too."

"I talked to Dr. Rolland and Deb here to get you all scheduled to work with me from now on." TJ continued. "I need a consistent research team. One that I can trust to determine what's going on with these so-called attacks."

"I'm confused. Weren't there attacks?" Mellie asked.

"There were shark incidents. When a dog bites, we don't call it a dog attack."

"So, you're saying the shark bit, but not necessarily attacked, right?" Mellie asked for more clarification, intent on learning the lingo and establishing her credibility. *Gotta talk the talk and walk the walk.*

"Correct. We don't know the shark attacked. All we really know is it bit the surfer and board. People say shark attack. That's a bias my work is attempting to clear up." TJ said. "Let's start the briefing on the work for this week. I'll be assigning your tasks."

21

"You think it will take all week, then?" Sandy asked.

"It will," Burt confirmed. "Truth be told, this work may last well beyond the summer. We're using *The Minnow* . I helped refit it for the HIMB. It's small, but big enough for our crew. It's seaworthy, equipped and ready to go."

"I need you all to know," Deb said, "you aren't here just because you're lab students. Burt and I, along with Dr. Rolland, vetted each of you thoroughly. This research falls under Dr. Rolland's domain. My understanding is that he selected everyone here based on their specialty studies. TJ here" — she poked him in the ribs — "reminded me again this morning that he needed an experienced crew for the tasks ahead. Although Mellie is new to the Pacific, she is specializing in tiger sharks and has considerable experience on the Atlantic Ocean. She, like the rest of you, has the skill set we require and need."

TJ took over then. "We'll need to survey the area, see if there's any more debris from the incident." He looked each of them straight in the eye, no traces of humor showing now. "You'll be playing detectives in more ways than one. I'll be dividing you to do various tasks. Some of the work will be tedious. Burt will interview the first responders."

"Deb, your team will talk with the press that covered the incident. Mellie will record the presence and activity of sharks using the data from the search grid I've sent to her tablet. I'll be collecting and analyzing the debris field."

"And Deb? Interview others in the area at the time. Sunbathers, swimmers, surfers, anyone you can. See if you have the specs for the bite patterns and fragments of teeth I gave you yesterday. Everybody capisce? We'll debrief back at The Wharf over a very late dinner."

At everyone's nod, they loaded the boat and set off for Maui.

After three hours, TJ pulled up to The Wharf on Maui to

allow Burt, Sandy, and Deb to retrieve Burt's jeep, which he apparently kept there so they could conduct their interviews. Each researcher had a tablet on which to record the results of their interviews. They agreed to meet up much later and grab dinner.

Mellie and TJ headed out to sea to search the site off Makena beach for more debris and hopefully information. They rode in comfortable companionship, making casual conversation.

"It seems like we're about nine hundred yards from the beach, am I right?" Mellie asked.

"Affirmative."

"Then we must be at the scene of the crime."

"We are."

"This looks like a popular site. You name it, people are doing it, even kite surfing."

"Good observation," TJ said. "Log that on your tablet. Can you make a table that shows date, time, and activities?"

"Do sharks bite?" she teased. "Of course, I can."

"Add the GPS data as well to another column," TJ directed. "While you're at it, remind me to have you upload the shark sighting data, so if we see any, we can chart it then and there."

"I don't have to remind you because Deb had me upload it before we set out. Burt, Sandy, me, you, we all have it."

"There is so much to be said for an experienced lab crew. Not that there isn't room in the program for the fieldwork we do with undergrads," he hastened to add.

"Good, because while I'm only a course away from graduation, I'm still officially an undergrad. I decided long before this outing to make myself indispensable and wanted. I'm extremely serious about a career here with tiger sharks. "

"Trust me," TJ said in a dry tone, "You're both."

His tone made Mellie wonder if there was more to what he was saying. *Could he want me? What? Mellie, look in the mirror, they all want you. The question was, did they ever want anything else?* She sighed. Her situation was kind of like the poor little rich girl thing. Her looks made desire almost a given, but that didn't necessarily lead to lasting commitment. Case in point—Wolfe. *Not him again.* She wished she could charge him rent for the space he occupied in her head. Perhaps she could rent it to TJ. *As if. Get real, girl. Focus.*

TJ grinned. "No problem. I'm told you have a great deal of fieldwork on the Atlantic, so you aren't really a rookie newbie."

"There's no such thing," she laughed.

"Sure, there is."

She countered. "Sure, and snipes do exist."

"On the north shore on Oahu, people go on snipe hunts all the time."

Not believing him for a moment, Mellie said, "They do not."

"Do too."

"Do not."

TJ's voice was firm, his expression serious. "I'll prove it and take you on a snipe hunt this weekend. Promise."

"Yeah, right."

"Saturday."

"Uh-huh," she said, not at all serious, and doubting more each minute.

"I will."

"Won't."

"Will. Wanna bet on it?"

"You are so on." Mellie had an idea of what she wanted when she won.

"Terms?" TJ asked.

"Windsurfing."

"You want to tandem with me?"

She jutted one hip out in a stance of defiance and derision.

"Hell no," she said. "I want you to teach me."

"How do you know I kiteboard?"

"I took one look. It was all it took, and then I knew." She smiled, feeling a tad bit devilish, too.

"There's a song that goes like that." TJ's face scrunched up like he was thinking hard.

"Which one?" she challenged.

"I'm thinking."

"Shouldn't this be on the tip of your tongue?" she asked. "You are a singer and all, right?"

"Yes, but I major in Big Band, only minor in Pop."

"Big Band major? Pop minor? How's that?"

"I have a double degree One in music, one in marine biology." He gave her a smirk. "You know, I believe you were a bit judgmental about me, and I should be insulted."

Mellie lifted her eyebrow. "Say what?"

"You must admit when you saw me, you automatically assumed I was just another cool surfer dude. One who strums a mean ukulele, with no brain, and certainly no degrees. Just another pretty face."

Her face must have given her away. "Well, that's true."

He laughed, then huffed, "That's why I should be insulted." Then he winked. "You didn't think I could possibly have a degree, much less several serious academic passions. I compose, write lyrics, and perform in addition to conducting research on sharks."

"You are quite talented and correct about my thinking. I was way off base," she admitted. "Am I forgiven a rookie mistake?" She smiled, batting her eyes playfully.

"You do know you look like a Basset hound when you do that, don't you?"

"But a cute Basset hound. Everyone loves Basset hounds, right?"

Out of the blue, he asked, "Do you believe in fairies, angels, and Menehune?"

I bet he's changing the subject as much to keep me talking as to get through his memory lapse about the Pop Music.

She chuckled. "Angels, yes. The rest not so much."

"Skeptic. So, you don't believe in the Hawaiian leprechauns either?"

She just looked at him. "Seriously?"

"Seriously. The Hawaiian tell of a race of little people, the Menehune, who worked by night and made what are called Menehune fishponds, so there."

"I'm going to Google that as soon as I get the chance."

He guffawed. "I'll get to say I told you so."

"We'll see about that."

"I'm so sure about it that I'll bet on it," TJ said, puffing out his chest and looking like a Hawaiian demi-god.

She hated to admit it, but his good looks, gorgeous body, and smarts made him much more appealing than she wished. She'd felt a zing ricochet through her body when she first saw him that morning.

He was beginning to make her aware of her girly parts with increasing frequency. She wasn't sure that was such a good thing after her misspent times with the men she had previously found attractive. She'd had enough of pretty boys to last her a lifetime. *I am so over men. Hotter than hell or not. I'm done with that. Fini.* "Really. Again? Another bet? What are the terms?"

"If I'm right, and I am" —he added a cocky grin—" dinner."

"Hey, I'm a student, remember? No job, no money."

"So am I," he said.

"Say what?"

"Okay. I'm a doctoral student, and I do have a job. Let's make it dinner at The Hat Check Lounge on Kalakaua Ave on Oahu. I have some pull there."

"Wait a minute. That's where you sing, isn't it?" Mellie asked.

"For my supper, sure. It's a nice place even you can afford."

"Sounds like a cheap date to me," she returned. Then realizing what she said, she blushed, adding, "But it's only a date if you lose."

"Call it what you want." His tone was smug. "You game?"

"You betcha," she said with equal force. "Bring it."

"I'll do better than that. Give me your pinky finger."

"I have another finger that'll work better to express my thoughts on the matter."

"Just stick it out."

She stuck out her tongue.

"Dangerous. Don't stick that out unless you intend to use it, and I know how you can."

She flushed and extended her pinky.

He linked his through hers and shook it. "Pinky promise."

"What? How old are you? Ten-years-old?"

He laughed, then sobered. "This is the most solemn of all promises. My grandmother taught me that, and, yes, I was ten at the time. I meant it then, and I mean it now. You have my word. It's a real date." He looked deeply into her eyes as he spoke.

Even though they were goofing around, Mellie knew he meant it.

Their exchange was cut short when suddenly TJ called, "Starboard side, your two o'clock."

Mellie had learned that sea positions were called according to the clock. Two o'clock meant look where the two on a clock would be. She looked.

A fourteen-foot shark breached the surface.

"Chart that. Record it. Hit that camera," TJ commanded as he grabbed his tablet.

Mellie recorded her findings, started the video, then sat in awe, watching the beautiful animal in the bright turquoise sea. Like the islands, the sea and the shark were each awe-inspiring.

She quivered with her excitement. "That's freakin' amazing!"

"Totally."

They spent a very productive day on the sparkling green-blue sea. They had anchored to eat lunch, and Mellie was overheating in the too warm sunshine. She removed her t-shirt, revealing a skimpy tankini top. Then she slipped off her shorts and headed to the edge of the boat to go for a swim.

TJ grabbed her and held her back. "No swimming. Not now, not here."

"Hey, I'm an accomplished swimmer, I'll have you know." She stood confidently, hands on hips. "And I'm hot."

"But that doesn't give you the right to swim in shark-infested waters." His gruff tone a sharp reminder.

"Oh. Jeez. My bad," she said with a shrug. "I'm simply hotter than hell."

He winked. "I noticed."

TJ walked over to some equipment, grabbed a small hose, and sprayed her. It was the hose used to keep sharks comfortable and wet when they were lifted from the ocean for testing and tagging.

"What the . . ." Mellie sputtered. "What do you think you're doing?"

"How about saving your life and cooling you off? Look." He pointed to the dorsal fin of a prowling shark near the boat. "I rest my case."

"Oops." Mellie shuddered.

"You'd be a mighty tempting morsel for that big kahuna."

"I suppose that makes you my hero."

"It's a tough job, but someone's got to do it." He smiled, breaking the tension. "Isn't there a reward for such selfless heroism?"

"Why, yes, sir, there is." She smiled sweetly. "Close your eyes, and you'll get it." Reaching into the remains of her lunch, she speared a piece of pineapple. "Ready?"

She got up close and personal, her body mere inches from his. Her fingertips traced his lips. When TJ's lips parted, she popped in the succulent pineapple.

"How was that?" she asked.

"Disappointing. After all, I did save your life."

"What more did you want?"

"This." He pulled her closer and kissed her.

She licked the remaining pineapple from his lips and nestled into his muscled chest, then suddenly took a huge step back.

"What's wrong?"

She grabbed the same hose he dosed her with and turned it on him. "That'll cool you off." Thinking of Wolfe and Nikki's talk of sexual harassment, Mellie gulped, "Can we get in trouble? Can this be considered sexual harassment?"

"What, kissing?"

"Uh-huh."

"What makes you think that?"

"My previous relationship with a professor. Should I disqualify myself from this team? I don't want to make trouble for you. And I don't want any harassment issues, either."

"I'm not your prof," he stated. "I don't even grade you. I just show you the ropes."

"And therein lies the rub. Oh, no, I didn't just say that. Pardon the pun."

"Okay. Here's what we do. On sea, pure professionalism. On land . . ."

He left the comment unfinished, but his expression promised things that made her insides shiver.

"Is that legal?"

"Don't know, but it's smart. I think that's how it works. I'm

29

new at this aspect. I'm a shark-incident researcher, a student just like you. Students can date. But we'll take precautions."

"Precautions? That's a bit presumptuous, don't you think?"

He laughed. "I love a girl with a sense of humor. We both do have a lot to lose."

"Okay," She agreed. "On land, yeah, on sea, not. Pinky promise."

"This is going to be a heck of a challenge," TJ complained.

"Why?"

"Because I want to do this again."

"You promised."

"It only takes effect thirty seconds after you pledge."

She slugged him.

And he looked like he was burning to kiss her again. "You know"—he tossed her the t-shirt and shorts—"you need to cover up."

"So I don't burn?" she asked.

"No. So I don't. Just looking at you makes me want much more than kisses."

Mellie ran her fingers along her sore lips. "Between you and the pineapple I've been eating, I don't dare indulge in either kisses or pineapple."

"Now, there's the rookie in you coming out again," he teased.

"Hey, are you bad-mouthing my kissing technique? Cuz that's just rude."

"Not hardly," he said, grabbing a piece of a plant from the specimens on board. He broke the plant, and a thick liquid spilled over his fingers.

"Come here," he directed.

When she was closer, he traced her lips with the liquid from the plant.

"Oh. That helps. What is it?"

"Aloe at its freshest. It beats *DryStick* anytime.'"

"Well, I won't always be on this research boat, so I'll have to get some aloe lip balm for times when you and your plant are unavailable."

"Damn shame," he muttered.

"What?"

"It's a damn shame kissing hurts, my wonder plant won't be around twenty-four-seven, and I can only kiss you on land."

They spent the rest of the day combing the seas, hoping to find the answers within its bounty. When it started to get dark, they headed back to The Wharf on Maui.

"Over here," Deb half rose from her seat to beckon them to the table.

Burt and Sandy were seated, throwing back ice cold Heinekens.

After everyone exchanged greetings and placed their orders, they began to debrief.

TJ started by reporting their findings. "Mellie and I spotted two tigers. The data on them has been uploaded to your tablets and is displayed and plotted on the map. While it's too soon to make claims, the sharks do seem to be appearing here more frequently than usual. Remember, sharks have the whole ocean to inhabit and hunt. I'd say the two we saw were in cruise mode. Mellie made a chart of everything she saw regarding human activity in the area. Share what you found, Mellie."

"You name it, it was all happening. There were a hundred people sunbathing and swimming. I counted a half dozen fishing from the jetty toward sunset. There was quite a bit of spear-fishing, too."

"Any numbers on that?" Burt asked.

"Four. It's on the chart that I sent to all of you. I named the

31

file The Wheaton Report."

TJ studied his tablet. "This table is clear and easy to understand. Good work." He nodded his approval.

Mellie beamed. "I thought the Excel spreadsheet, with some tweaks, would make it user-friendly."

Sandy checked the table Mellie designed. "I see there were over a dozen surfers. And eight windsurfing. Wow! That has to mean something."

"Human activity appears to be a factor," TJ stated.

"Easy prey," Deb said. "More people in the water, more opportunities for contact."

"I think the spear-fishing has a lot to do with the bite incident," Burt said. "I talked with the first responders, and they seemed to agree. The bite got the victim on the foot."

"That's because he was in the same vicinity as the spear fishermen, I bet," Sandy added.

"There were two incidents reported. Both bitten on the foot." Burt checked his data. "The first one was the surfer. The other was in a kayak, and he was dangling his foot overboard."

"Why would he do that?" Mellie said aghast.

"Some people have no sense, no respect for the ocean, and what's in it. There are tales of incidents that occurred during pupping season. What do they expect?" Burt asked.

"The Hawaiian elders avoided the ocean during the winter, which is prime pup time. They spread the word to their children. We have to do a better job educating people." Deb added.

"What did you find on the board and bite analysis, Deb?" TJ asked.

"One, the bite pattern on the board shows it was a tiger about fourteen to sixteen feet. The embedded tooth shows the same."

"That could have been the first shark we saw," Mellie deduced.

"It might have been the one who could have eaten you for lunch, too," TJ reminded her.

A short discussion about safety followed.

Mellie blushed with embarrassment. "My bad. Won't happen again."

"Rookie mistake," Deb said with a sympathetic tone. "You aren't the first."

"It's time to turn this information over to the State of Hawaii's Division of Aquatic Resources," TJ said. "HIMB's research doesn't extend beyond this."

"How's that?" Mellie asked, bemused. "This is research."

"But the HIMB concentrates almost exclusively on biological research, water quality, parasites, population number, and food source. I was fortunate that they approved my proposal as it is. I'm going to get with some resident research guys on Maui to help."

"Does this mean this project won't take all summer?" Sandy queried.

"Oh, no. We just have to do a lot more biological observations is all," TJ promised." "That's going to take time."

They finished their dinner and headed back to the boat. The trip home was beautiful. The seas were calm, the stars bright, and all was well.

It was late when they reached Oahu. There was a flurry of activity as they straightened up the boat, gathered their things, and left for home. They were all whipped. Mellie gave a collective wave and was about to leave when TJ stopped her.

"Tomorrow, nine a.m."

"No crack of dawn?" Mellie asked, relieved beyond measure.

"Not this time," TJ assured. "No kiss good night?"

Smiling she shook her head. "Not this time."

"What? We're on land."

"So we are." She walked over to where he was standing. Noting the crew was disbanding and not paying attention, she moved intending to give him a chaste peck on the cheek, but his strong arms reached out and grabbed her close.

"Let's see if it's better on land." He gave her a scorching kiss. "Hmm, not enough data." And he kissed her again.

"Whoa, boy," Mellie pushed away. "I'd say we need more data, but that's it for now." She walked away.

Mellie left for home, longing for more and feeling fairly confident TJ did, too. *Not jumping in with both feet this time. Gonna take things slow.*

Chapter Four: Stupid Rules

TJ and the crew met at nine a.m., but Mellie had been on his mind all night. When he saw her the next morning, he approached her with a wink and a grin. "We're on land."

"Not gonna happen, big guy."

"I wish I could pull rank."

"Been there, done that." Her voice was firm. "I'm off the market and not looking for love in all the wrong places."

"I could say that sounds like a corny country song." TJ was a tad disappointed *No, scratch that thought, majorly disappointed.* "You know what they say if the song fits . . ."

"Nobody says that."

TJ thrust his chest out. "I just did."

"Have it your way."

"Okay," Mellie said, smirking. She was obviously trying hard not to laugh at their absurd banter.

"Does that mean I get my kiss?"

"No. It means let's get to work."

"Kill joy."

"I've been called worse."

"I hope not."

"I have lousy taste in men."

"You have to risk it to get the biscuit," TJ reminded her.

"Do you even know how lame that sounds?" she countered. "Who says that?"

"Jimmy Fallon, among others."

"Oh. Then it must not be lame."

"If the biscuit fits . . ."

"Don't even try to finish that thought. That *would* be considered harassment."

As TJ bantered with Mellie, the rest of the crew was loading equipment. He and Mellie each grabbed a side of a dinghy to load it on board. This trip they were bringing two dinghies with small outboard motors.

Deb would handle the main boat, running data and observing.

Sandy and Burt would take a dingy and observe the left quadrant, and TJ and Mellie would cover the Makena beach site. They all had their tablets, which were updated and set to go.

Once they were in their own dingy, TJ couldn't help but notice Mellie's white, long sleeved top tied under her very full breasts, baring her midriff. It made it difficult to concentrate.

"I'd offer to put sunblock on your back. Uh, purely professional non-harassment, of course, but you'd have to remove your . . . ah . . . top."

"Thanks. I think. But I'm not wearing anything underneath today."

"Then by all means, you should remove it. It's my duty as crew captain to ensure your safety. This tropical sun burns you know."

She giggled.

"You know," he continued, "I could get those hard to reach places. Your legs. Oh, and your arms. Your toes."

"My toes?"

"Oh, yes, toes easily burn, and you don't want that."

She lifted her foot, waving it. "I'm wearing my water shoes, so no need. Sorry."

"Not as sorry as you'll be. You're the one missing a mighty good foot massage."

Mellie laughed out right at that and continued in a teasing

vein. "How about my midriff?"

"Definitely that."

"I can be helpful, too. I can do your back. Your legs. Your chest." She giggled. "Your toes."

"Be my guest," TJ exclaimed happily all too willing. He raised his foot and wiggled his toes.

Instead Mellie shoved his foot aside and grabbed the sunblock to spread it on his chest.

His muscles twitched under her touch, and a jolt shot through him. But it was nothing compared to the bolt of lightning sensation that followed. He knew she had to feel it, too. Her body looked sizzling, after all.

She stopped abruptly. "This isn't a good idea."

"Au contraire. It's a great idea."

From the confused expression on Mellie's face, TJ had to wonder what she was thinking. Part of her seemed to want to get into it with him right there, right now, while her other half seemed like she wanted no part of him.

Meanwhile TJ was trying vainly to tame his desires. *What am I, superman? I'm only human. Hot damn and the horse passion rode in on. I want to do more than research with Mellie.* "Stupid policy."

Mellie bit her lips. "Ouch."

TJ figured her lips were still tender from sun and pineapple exposure from the day before. *She would taste so good. Pineapple juice would taste like sunshine, but instead of in a glass, it would be on her full sensuous lips.*

"I can kiss them and make them all better," he reminded her.

TJ watched in fascination as Mellie whipped out her lip balm and applied it to her luscious lips. She looked like a model for a lipstick commercial when she outlined them with aloe two or three times.

TJ's gaze followed her movements, knowing he would give anything to do that with his tongue. He felt the stirrings down below and wished he hadn't opened this line of discussion.

Clearing his throat, he said, "You take fore, and I'll take aft. We are looking for all things shark, and all the things listed on *The Wheaton Report*."

"Aye, aye, *El Capitan*."

He wished he weren't captain, wished they were ashore where he could delight them both. He shifted in his seat and handed her the binoculars. It was pure temptation to sit so close to her. It became agonizing when she'd periodically re-apply the sunblock to her exposed flesh.

Neither moved in any direction that would lead to a sensual overload, but he was increasingly aware of her nearness. He knew she felt the pull, too. Her movements, shying away, confirmed his speculation.

By late afternoon, they returned to the main boat.

CHAPTER FIVE: ON THE SEA

The days conducting research on the ocean seemed to melt slowly into each other. Mellie just wanted TJ to melt into her, but she stuck to her plan to take things slow.

The daily routine began to follow a predictable pattern. Each team knew their roles, and they all set out to gather as much data as possible.

This trip out, TJ and Mellie were going to check food sources in the vicinity. They would be scuba diving to collect both water samples at different depths and try to get numbers on the available food nearby. They wondered whether that was what was drawing the sharks to the area.

After they donned their gear, TJ sat on the edge and flipped off the dinghy just like they did on television.

Mellie followed suit. Soon, she was enchanted by the underwater world surrounding her. Beautiful fish were everywhere.

TJ gestured to her, pointing to her left when a school of clownfish swam past.

She tried to smile, then laughed to herself because the facemasks didn't leave much room for reading facial expressions or emotions. *TJ must think my efforts to convey my feelings were hilarious.* Mellie tried elaborate eye contact, but that only seemed to distract TJ from his work.

At that moment, all TJ could think of was wanting to be the cause of the expression of satisfaction on Mellie's face. The wetsuit she wore displayed every curve she had, and she looked very sexy as she swam the grid gathering data. He tried hard to keep his mind off her and on his work, but that was proving to be impossible. Each encounter he had with her just made the ache in his loins worse.

He was glad when they stripped off the wetsuits, which he feared made his hard-on all too visible. It didn't seem to help much, so he changed into bulky but roomy cargo shorts to mislead the eye, or at least he hoped they would.

Mellie had taken to wearing a bikini top with a sleeveless, loose skimpy over-blouse. Every time she moved, her breasts created another distraction. She paired the top with fashionable cut-off jean shorts, which rode high on her tanned long-legs.

Since TJ's shorts managed to camouflage the bulge in his pants, he chose to go shirtless. He hoped his build was causing some similar stirrings in Mellie's stomach, and deep in her pelvis, too, if he was being honest.

Her hands trembled on his skin when TJ asked her to apply sunblock.

"You should know better," she scolded as her fingertips traced the contours of his back's muscles. "You're smart enough to wear a hat, but going bare chested is pushing it. You need to cover up."

"Look who's talking," he said with a leer, taking that moment to feast his eyes on her too-exposed skin.

"Touché." She turned to her duffle bag and pulled out a sun-blocking long-sleeved Mother Hubbard type cover-up. "Is this better?"

"Depends on how you define better."

As they were sorting water samples, one of the container tubes began to fall. They both grabbed for it at the same time. When their hands touched, bare skin to bare skin, TJ startled. He got his proof that Mellie felt the same thing when their gazes locked and they stared at each other as a strong fiery current flashed between them. TJ drew his hand back, but it was evident they were both shaken by the strength of the pull between them.

For the next week, each day that they worked together they because easier and more comfortable with the routine. For TJ, the problem was the sexual tension that began to invade their work zone. It was harder and more difficult keeping true to their *on water on land* agreement. They continued working like that throughout the week until they returned to shore Friday night.

TJ reminded her about the snipe hunt he'd promised for Saturday. "I'll use Mark's sailboat and —"

"Wait a minute. Mark has a sailboat?" Mellie asked with an incredulous tone. "Since when?"

"You should know, he's your brother."

" He doesn't tell me everything," Mellie muttered.

"He's male. He has a lot of toys. You know he has a helicopter, right?"

"No. Does he have a jet ski and windsurf board?" she asked.

"I wouldn't be surprised, but I don't know all of it. I met him through my work at the *Hat Check.* He loves that place. I get some gigs from him, and I've crewed with him. He has a small sloop, which I've borrowed for tomorrow."

"And he approves of you taking me snipe hunting?" she asked, sounding somewhat skeptical.

TJ grinned. "Some things Mark has no need to know. Tell you what, let's make a day out of it. I'll bring a picnic supper, then the hunt takes place at the Kualoa Ranch about eight p.m. After, we'll have a moonlight sail home."

"This will make you be easy pickings, since there's no such thing as a snipe."

He held his ground. "Is too."

"Is not."

He thrust his chest forward. "Game on."

"Bring it."

TJ had worked it out with Sam Martin, the owner of *The Hat Check Lounge,* to take the weekend off. He had already talked to his band, and Skip would take his place, doing double duty singing and playing keyboard. Maxine, the cook and only mother figure in his life, could refuse him nothing, so she prepared a picnic supper for them. Everything was set.

CHAPTER SIX: SAILING

TJ readied his motor bike after arranging to meet Mellie outside the lounge. Mellie had seen him ride off many times, and he'd told her they would be using his bike to get to the harbor where Mark's boat was berthed.

He chuckled as he pulled in front of *Hat Check* when Mellie grabbed her neon yellow helmet, which matched her capris and tank top. She jumped on the back of his bike, snuggling her girlie parts to his backside. He was affected by her close proximity, and wondered if she felt it, too.

When they reached the marina, TJ helped Mellie dismount and attached their helmets to the bike. He led her to Mark's boat slip and helped her on board. In minutes, he maneuvered the boat away from the pier and headed for Kualoa Ranch.

Mellie put her fingers in her mouth and whistled—like many men wished they could—as she looked around the sloop. "Oh brother, she's beautiful."

"*Beautiful Dreamer* is one sweet boat all right"

"One can't help having sweet dreams with a boat like this."

"We could test that theory. This boat has a double berth down below. There's even a galley for morning coffee."

"In your dreams, buster. That is sooo not happening."

"But it could. You've but to say the word."

"Is that all it takes? One word?"

He promised, making a shaka sign. "Say yes. One word will make that bed sing with the beautiful music we'd make."

She smiled. "Lame attempt. Wait for it."

He stopped. "Well? What's it gonna be? One word only."

She gave him a saucy look. "No."

"Major buzzkill." He gave her a lopsided grin. "You'll be soorry," he added in a childish, singsong voice.

Awhile into the trip, TJ dropped anchor and broke out the picnic supper. They feasted on cold fried chicken, island macaroni salad, a fruit salad—with no pineapple—and Heinekens.

"We could have driven here," TJ said between bites, "but this is such a beautiful ride by sea, I couldn't resist."

Mellie just smiled.

Was she glad they didn't use the bike? Could her nether parts take that close contact much longer? The vibrations alone made my body sing.

The day was perfect. TJ and Mellie didn't talk all that much as they sailed along the coastline. He was busy operating the boat while Mellie following the simple commands he'd issued.

He'd caught Mellie admiring the view several times as the boat glided over the calm waters. It was one thing to see the islands from the air, another from the shore. But seeing the coastline from the boat was beyond anything most had ever seen or imagined.

"This view is unbelievable. This is truly paradise," Mellie said, breaking the silence.

"Wait until you see the Na Pali Coast along the north west coast of Kauai. It's a showstopper. Leaves you breathless. It's very dangerous to sail there. We'd need a much larger boat and more crew. It'd be a great place to visit on a honeymoon."

He had to smile when Mellie abruptly changed the subject. She asked, "What mountains were those we just passed?"

"They're the Ko'olau Mountains."

Mellie bit her lip. "The view from here makes me feel like crying."

"Hawaii has that effect on people. When the wind is right,

you feel like you're flying over the water. The beauty just never stops. Sort of like you."

Her cheeks colored a bit. "Me?"

"Yes, you. You are as beautiful as this ocean, that island, those mountains. You are every man's dream."

"Tell that to Wolfe." She clarified, "My ex."

"Were you" — he made air quotes — "in love?"

"I thought so, but now . . . Not so much."

"Did you think the relationship was going to end happily ever after?"

"We weren't going there. I had school to finish. I wasn't ready, but I probably had some hopes in that direction. What about you? Was the *M* word in your vocabulary?"

"Not after I failed the *C* word."

"I'm sorry, *C word*?"

He choked the on the word. "Commitment."

Mellie laughed.

TJ paused for a brief second. *I need to find out more about this dude . . . this wolf man.* "I'm sorry he hurt you, but I'm not sorry you kicked him to the curb. You deserve better than that. If he was a catch, you'd have kept him, but you didn't. That tells me he's what my grandmother would call a *no-count*."

"Say again, a what?"

"A *no-count*, he's worthless, doesn't even count."

"Thanks. I think I'd like your grandmother"

"You'd love her. Everyone did, not just me and Gramps."

"Do they live here or on the mainland?"

"Sadly, no. They both passed."

"I'm sorry. Parents?"

"One died of a drug overdose, good ole Mom. The other never stuck around."

"What happened to you?"

"Gram and Gramps raised me until they passed. Then it was a series of foster homes. Kids in their teens aren't very adoptable. When I aged out of the system, I entered the armed forces. That's how I ended up here with a VA scholarship. Now you know my life's story. What about yours?"

"Parents died. Mom died of cancer. Dad? Some say a broken heart killed him. Mark raised me."

"Love life?"

"Another short story. Rich was high school. Wolfe, college. Now? Footloose and fancy free . . . and not interested," Mellie said. "Now, your turn."

"Nothing to tell. The usual boy meets girl. Girl dumps boy during a tour of duty. Boy signs off on all things love."

"I told you my story."

"Obviously there's more to the story," TJ said. "Spill."

"Not much more worth telling."

"Anyone who meets you soon learns you're not only pretty, but you are pretty smart, too. I'll bet a lot goes on in that head of yours. And there's more than meets the eye here."

Mellie didn't take his bait. Instead of responding to his queries she chose to banter.

"Just pretty smart?" she teased.

"Brilliant from your mind to your smile."

"Hm, you're not half bad yourself, and I can see by how you talk that you must write some killer songs. I've heard you sing, remember. I loved the lyrics to *Second Chances*. That song made me cry."

"It moved me, too. That was commissioned specifically for Chance and Caren."

The wind kicked up, and it was time to concentrate on boating again. They couldn't continue their conversation, so they sailed on in perfect harmony over the deep, bluer than blue sea.

CHAPTER SEVEN: IN THE JUNGLE

Once they reached Kualoa, TJ called the ranch shuttle, which picked them up and drove them to the snipe hunt site. There were about twenty people, mostly couples. Those that came alone were assigned a partner.

Hank Hauna, dressed in camouflage and holding many similar print vests, said, "Aloha, welcome to our ranch and grounds. This is a huge place, with some sections that are perfect for ATV rides and fishing. It also includes sites for many popular movies, such as *Pearl Harbor* and *Lost*. We are taking you into that section of jungle, because the snipe love a rain forest habitat. You'll each get some equipment, and you'll need a camouflage vest so you can sneak up on these shy animals."

These were distributed to the group by assistants as he spoke.

Mellie raised her hand. "Pardon the interruption, but what do they look like. Do you have a photo?"

Hank cleared his throat, looking embarrassed. "So far, no one knows exactly how they look. They're very adept at hiding from predators." Gesturing with both hands he said, "They are about yay high, weigh about five pounds and are green-black. Very similar to the vest you're wearing. They're very shy, and when startled they can be aggressive. We have had little success in capturing them, but with a full super moon, the odds are on our side. They mate during the full moon, so you have picked a great night to hunt. When the moon's out, they get a little looney, pardon the pun.

"Sort of like humans, then," TJ adlibbed as the hunters chuckled.

Hank just smiled and went on with the instructions. "Leah and Liana will apply your camouflage makeup so you won't be as visible to the snipe, who are said to have keen eyesight. Any questions?"

Mellie's hand shot up again. "Are we going out in the jungle totally alone?"

"Oh no, we'll be in the field with you, but we're not escorting you. Your miner helmets are equipped not only with headlights but also with GPS locators. We don't want to stage another episode of *Lost*."

"What will we be using to catch the snipes?" another hunter asked.

"For your protection, you will wear soccer pads for your legs. These are land-loving beasts, but they can take flight. That means you'll need these." He gestured to his assistants.

While shin guards were distributed and donned, more assistants passed out butterfly nets to catch the elusive snipe. Others handed everyone canvas sacks to hold them.

"Follow me, and we'll lead you to various quadrants to hunt."

The group shuffled nervously, but everyone seemed excited.

"Sometimes the best way to hunt snipe is to beat the bushes to flush them out." Hank demonstrated, but no snipe emerged. "Let's say I flushed one out. Your partner will use the net to catch them if they fly or scoot, then slide them into the sack. As soon as you catch one, return here to base camp and we'll weigh it, photograph it, and give you the trophy. So far no one has won. Decide who will do what and we'll begin."

"I still don't know what I'm really looking for," Mellie grumbled but set off with TJ in the lead.

She was shushed by someone behind her.

Knowing Mellie a little better now, TJ would almost bet she was thinking something along the lines of *Who made you the snipe police? Shushing moi? How dare she?*

Mellie held her peace, but thunder crossed her face.

TJ bit back a laugh.

Soon they were in dense underbrush with oversized ferns. It was quite humid, and everyone was forced into a crouched position as they literally beat the bushes. Squeals and peals of laughter rang out as partners were snatched by the wildly flying nets. People tended to jump the gun when it was their partner that moved a bush, not a snipe. Occasionally a bat flew out and someone would squeal.

A movement along the ground caused Mellie to stop cold. A jungle rat scurried out. She shuddered.

"Wait! I'll save you, fair damsel." TJ scooped her up in his arms he-man style.

"Put me down, you ape," was Mellie's barely audible response. "Between the rat and you, I wasn't sure which to tackle first." She laughed, but it was a little shaky."

TJ set her down, reluctantly, and they continued the hunt.

"I feel ridiculous." Mellie said from a crouched position.

"C'mere then," TJ coaxed.

When she rose, he swung his net over her and drew her in for a kiss. With her body pressed close to his, he felt her pulse quicken, and his body responded. He set her back and gruffly said "Over there! I see something! Snipe!"

They both turned to look when their helmets collided.

Mellie reeled back. "So far the only thing we've caught is each other. You knocked my helmet off."

"I'd like to knock your socks off, and a few other unnecessary pieces of clothing. There are worse things that could happen," TJ responded.

"Like what?" Mellie asked.

"We could get squeezed by a boa constrictor."

Mellie wasn't having it. "There are no boas here and no snakes on Hawaii. You've got your habitats wrong."

TJ pounced, squeezing her tightly. "Look out! Don't look now, but a big, fat boa has you clutched inside his . . . uh . . . clutches."

They rolled around laughing. Then TJ stopped, stunned by the electricity jolting through him. They untangled themselves, dusted themselves off, smiled sheepishly, and then . . .

"Do you hear anything?" Mellie whispered. "Do you hear the others?"

He paused to listen. "Now that you mention it, no."

"Not to worry, we've got GPS trackers, remember?" she said.

TJ checked his helmet. "Mine's gone. Must have dislodged when our head bump." He began scrambling, trying to find the missing pieces.

Mellie found a cracked sensor. "Great! We're lost on the set of *Lost*. You weren't a boy scout, were you?"

"Nope, but I do camp. On my income, it's the only way I can manage some cheap entertainment."

"Can we make a fire?"

"If you want me to sing around a campfire, just say so," TJ teased.

"Yuck. Yuck. Very funny. I thought the smoke might draw their attention, then Hank & Company could find us."

"In a forest? We'd probably burn it down and they'll find our scorched remains. Do you have any matches?"

"What? You just said we'd burn the place down, and no, I don't, do you?" Mellie brushed a hand across her brow leaving a streak of dirt. She looked sweaty and somewhat peeved. "If we didn't stop to kiss . . . If you weren't such a goof, we might have paid more attention to the mission or at least our surroundings. No matches then?"

"No. Do you have a magnifying glass?"

"No, do you? What are you going to use for sunlight?"

"Super moon light."

Mellie was miffed and looked hot, too. "You're a scientist. Aren't magnifying glasses standard equipment?"

"So are you," TJ responded. He began walking around looking at the ground.

Mellie tapped her foot impatiently. "Now what are you doing? I'm through hunting for non-existent snipe."

"I'm looking for a trail. Hank knows this area. They hunt here all the time. Basic rules of hiking are to stay together and stay on the trail. That means you need to stick to me like glue." Once again, he grabbed her close. "You know what, Virginia, snipes do exist. We just didn't find any. But we found each other." He gave her a long, slow, deliberate kiss, and eased his hands under her shirt exploring her treasures.

"*We* weren't lost."

"We are now." He went in for another kiss and caress of her silky, soft flesh.

"You have got to grow up and be serious," she grumbled but moved further into the protective circle of his arms.

"We have no choice. We'll stay put until they find us. Body heat will keep us warm," he said, drawing her even closer.

"Ha. Ha. This is Hawaii. It's in the seventies."

"You can't be too careful," he noted.

"Do you have your cell?"

"No bars. You?"

"Ditto."

TJ looked skyward. "Well, the moon is pretty"

They stayed put and huddled close.

"I'll keep you safe," he murmured.

"Promises, promises," Mellie said." "That's what they all say."

"When I promise, I come through," he said, serious now. "Promises reveal a person's character. You break it, you show a character flaw. I'm not into flaws. When I say I promise, I mean it."

"Ah, now I see. Moonlight promises on the beach. I love it, even when I don't buy it," Mellie said with a heavy dose of skepticism. "Not something that you can really trust."

"You can if I'm the one doing the promising. I don't lie. I don't cheat. Never have, never will. And . . . I won't deliberately hurt you. You have my word."

CHAPTER EIGHT: LOST

The hunt was officially over. Everyone had arrived back at the base camp comparing notes and catches. No one had caught anything, which was typical. But when Hank did a head count, it was apparent who was missing. The crew waved the others off.

"Which quadrant were they assigned? "Hank asked.

"Omega."

"Of course, they were. Alpha would be too easy. We'll have to go in. Even with this moon they might not make it in for hours. Check the other quadrants to be on the safe side. Greg and I will head to Omega."

They roared off in their ATVs.

TJ felt fortunate that things were going well for Mellie and him. The night, while muggy, was not cool enough to endanger them. The biggest threat would have been hiking in the wrong direction or tripping and injuring themselves due to the elaborate root system of the trees and plants native to the rainforest.

They had spent most of their time making out. Just when things were beginning to heat up nicely, they heard the roar of the ATVs and jumped to their feet, brushing themselves off and rearranging clothing.

Bright lights blinded him momentarily, and he raised a hand to lessen the glare and learn who was there.

Hank!

The man pulled out his radio and announced, "Two pack-ages found. No worse for wear. All units in. We are heading for base. Copy that?"

"Roger that. Units heading for base," Greg responded.

TJ and Mellie gratefully climbed into the vehicle, where they had a bumpy and harrowing ride back to base.

"We'd have never found our way," Mellie said. "I'm so glad you found us. How on earth did you do that?"

"We did it the old-fashion way. A full quadrant search and rescue," Hank said.

"Mahalo," TJ said. "There was loads of drama but no snipe. We'll have to try, try, and try again."

"No, we won't," Mellie groused.

"Will."

"Won't."

"What are you two? Six years old?"

Relief and laughter overwhelmed them both.

TJ was dizzy from their experience and the heavy petting, but decided it was one of the best times he's ever had.

Liana handed them some wipes as they removed their bro-ken helmets, vests, and shin pads. TJ felt sweaty and grimy. They wiped their faces, mainly succeeding in smearing the grime.

When they got back to the boat, they decided to go for a swim. Unfortunately—or fortunately in TJ's mind—neither had brought suits, so they skinny-dipped.

"We're *at sea*, we can't . . . uh . . . connect," Mellie primly reminded him.

"We're dressed for the occasion. I'd say, it's a shame to pass up this opportunity."

They frolicked in the ocean, swimming in for close body contact then away again. A lot of kissing happened. They were playing a game of water tag, which TJ threw, preferring to get caught when Mellie stopped and pulled back.

"This is not safe," Mellie said.

"Are you afraid of sharks?"

"No. I'm afraid of unsafe sex."

"I have a fix for that," TJ said. "On board. I have protection. And there's a bed below."

"So, you're prepared for sex but not for getting lost. Hmmm, pretty convenient."

They climbed aboard and commenced with a highly personal drying off with a towel dance. TJ included kisses to each and every available spot he could reach on Mellie's body, and she returned the favor. After what felt like an eternity, they somehow made it below deck and collapsed on the small but comfortable berth. *I can't believe this is happening. She is so spectacular. She wants me! Unbelievable. How did I get so lucky?*

TJ did not know the answer—but he thanked every saint he had ever heard of. He was a bit leery when it came to thanking God because they were breaking rules right and left. But this felt so very right. If it was wrong, he didn't want to be right. This was no casual romp in the hay. He wanted this coming together to be meaningful and not just red-hot passion. The lushness of her breasts and the way they heaved as her excitement built each time he touched another exquisite part of her excited him in ways he had never, ever experienced.

He could see she was on fire, and so was he, to the point he thought he would explode. *Not yet. Whoa boy, slow down.*

But the hot trail of kisses that Mellie rained down his body would not allow the swell of sensation to do anything but hasten the fever in his blood. *I'm trying to take my time. I really am. But what am I, superman? She's every dream I ever had. Every fantasy come to life.*

She was on top, but he rolled her beneath him. He kissed the tender side of her jawbone to her ear and continued down to her collarbone.

She squealed and squirmed beneath the onslaught of his kisses. He wanted it to be good for her. Each touch, regardless of who touched whom, made him ignite even further. But when he tugged one beautiful large throbbing nipple into his mouth while caressing the other, he reached his limit. He simply could not take it anymore. He had to have her. He reached for the condom, but she stayed his hand.

"Let me," she purred. "Let me help."

The cool lubrication of the condom and the heat of her hand drove him absolutely insane. The condom on, he pulled her astride him and gave her what he hoped was a thrilling ride. He drank in the fullness of her luscious breasts as he once again sucked her delectable nipples into his mouth.

She let out a sigh and threw her head back as he drove into her. She bucked but held fast. All too soon, she collapsed against him and slowly rolled off.

He scooped her into a cuddle and drowned in the intoxicating scent and feel of her. "I hope that was okay for you." He drew her, if possible, even closer to him.

She smiled at him, her hair wild and tousled against full breasts as she drew the sheet around them. "Not enough data to make any solid conclusions."

He laughed. That was one theory he would be happy to test again and again. "We'll have to conduct more research then. No doubt about it."

"If we can repeat the test, then we'll be closer to the truth."

Head resting on his elbow, he cocked an eyebrow. "You game?" Hope bloomed in his chest.

"Set," she said.

Mellie jumped out of bed, grabbing the pillow and sheet as she ran lightly but quickly up the stairs and to the deck. TJ was hot on her trail. She threw the sheet and pillow onto the deck and lay there, gazing up at him. Above them, stars hung in the sky like a hundred crystal chandeliers as the full, super moon shone brightly down on them.

TJ pounced. "And match. Let the game begin."

There under that star strewn sky, they tested the theory once more.

When they were done, Mellie sighed softly, snuggled up to his side, and murmured, "Not enough data."

Seriously? Again? TJ was young and virile, but he was genuinely whipped.

"Mmm hmm . . ." she responded on a sigh, followed by soft, even breathing. A sure sign she'd fallen asleep.

Whew. I don't know if I could have kept up with her. He went below and gathered another pillow and a light blanket. He lay down beside her, threw the blanket over them both, and thanked his lucky stars as the gentle waves rocked him to sleep.

Mellie woke to the sounds of waves hitting the boat, gulls crying, the sun shining, and the aromas of bacon frying and coffee brewing. She gathered the sheets around her, making a *pareo* out of it. She tied the ends together under her breasts and went below.

"Good morning, sunshine," TJ greeted, handing her a glass of orange juice.

"Fresh squeezed?"

"I wish," he said holding up an eight-ounce serving bottle. "We can pretend."

"Pretending is good. And so is this juice."

"Ready for some breakfast?"

"If you're doing the cooking, then aye, aye, sir, I am." She gave him a mock salute. "I'm not a cook, but I can do toast."

"Have at it," he said, waving the way to the toaster with a flourish. "How do you like your eggs?"

"Over easy."

TJ cracked the eggs, then stared at them with a frown. "Scrambled? cuz I just put my thumb through your yolk. You shouldn't go around looking so good this early in the morning."

She giggled. "Scrambled's fine. No problem."

They ate in companionable silence. There was no awkward morning after. Mellie usually didn't spend the night with a guy, but these circumstances seemed perfect. Tailor-made, in fact. It was easy to be with TJ.

Clearly, she was at ease with him. He was not only easy on the eyes, but he was also comfortable in his own skin. And way comfortable being inside hers.

They cleaned up after breakfast, and Mellie gathered the bedding, putting it aside so it could be laundered. "Did Mark stuff the larder, or was that your doing too?

"Mine. This is a full-service establishment."

Mellie picked up on that and cozied up to him with a purr. "So I've found."

"Careful what you do," TJ said. "That could lead us into more research."

"Is that such a bad thing?"

"No," he said, kissing her. "It's a very good thing."

With that, he untied her make-shift gown and pulled her close. His tongue traced the contours of her mouth while his hands stroked her backside.

She was wet and ready for him instantly.

He pinned her to the wall and after some sound, serious kissing and heart stopping touching and caressing, he put on a condom. He raised her leg over his shoulder and entered her. Afraid her quaking legs would buckle, he eased them back to the stripped bed.

She spread the sheet over the bed, exposing a set of hips that made TJ react. His rod twitched and rose. He moved onto the bed and entered from behind. Mellie knelt as his hands fondled her breasts. She leaned her head back against his muscular chest and sighed.

When they were done, they each took a shower.TJ looked like he wanted to join her as he moved in her direction. Then she heard him swear.

" Son of a bitch. No condoms!"

As she left the shower, she saw him adjust the water to cold.

As TJ sailed them back to the harbor, Mellie noticed a group on the beach conducting Sunday services. They were situated between the boat slip and the parking lot.

"Do you mind if we join them?" TJ asked.

"No, but I kinda feel like a Saturday sinner," she admitted sheepishly.

"Then Sunday forgiveness is all you need. But seriously, God is about love, not Old Testament judgment. I feel very close to God when I'm out on the water, so Mass on the ocean does it for me."

"You're not suffering *Catholic guilt* then?"

"Nope. You?"

"I'm not Catholic so, no." she smiled. "I like the idea of a beach church kind of guy, though."

After the service, Mellie rode tandem on TJ's bike back to her place. When she got off, she said, "Time to pay up."

"What?"

"The snipe bet. I won."

"No, you didn't. I did."

"You think you won because of our make-out fest, but I was right. There are no such things as snipes. So, pay up. Teach me to windsurf."

"I say we go out hunting again. And again, and again. Until we prove I'm right."

Mellie laughed. "And I say, time to windsurf."

"How about I pick you up in say an hour and the lessons will begin?"

Mellie agreed, and went into her condo to change into her swimsuit, adding a cover-up that protected her arms and reached her knees. She pulled her hair into a ponytail and placed a Detroit Tigers baseball hat on her head, drawing her tail through the opening in the back. She packed her beach bag, added some condoms — just in case — grabbed two bottles of cold water, and waited for TJ's arrival. In the meantime, she checked her email. It was mostly the usual advertisements, jokes that made the email circuit, and chain email, which are typically spam. Then she spotted two that demanded her attention.

To: Mellie Wheaton
From: Nikki
Subject: Plans and arrival times
Hi, haven't heard from you lately but we're getting close to zero hour. I only have a few single girl days left. Mark and I are having two wedding ceremonies. One here at home and the other at the Moana Surf. Would you be my island Maid of Honor? Say yes. It'll be fun. Mark and I have been through wedding planning with my sister's wedding, so we have everything covered. The emerald green dress you wore to Caren's wedding will be perfect. We'll be arriving two weeks from tomorrow so we can take care of any last-minute needs. Say yes or I'll be forced to guilt you into it.
Xo
Nikki.

To: Nikki
From: Mellie Wheaton
Subject: YES!!!!!
Nikki,
YES! YES! YES!!!!! See you soon. Will you be staying here?

Hugs
Mellie

The second email was from Mark.

To: Mellie Wheaton
From: Mark
Subject: Coming Soon
Arriving Honolulu International airport in two weeks for wedding. Bringing Nikki, Gus and Daisy. No need for pick up. Lamina Limo Service will meet us. Should be at the condo at eighteen hundred hours. Behave. Mark

Yikes! Eighteen hundred hours. Who does he think he is? Captain Crunch? She chuckled when she thought of her recent escapades with TJ, which showed no signs of letting up. She didn't stop to figure out what time eighteen hundred hours was.

Chapter Nine: Time's Up

TJ approached the Aloha Towers Condominium Complex. He took the elevator to the eight floor, where Mellie lived, and rang the bell.

When she opened the door he whistled. He wasn't quite sure if he was whistling at her, the condo, or the view. They were all whistle worthy.

"Check it out!" He scoped out his surroundings. "This is one heck of a place. That view is fabulous." He pulled Mellie in for an open-mouthed, heart stopping kiss.

As before, she gave as good as she got, and he could feel himself rise to the occasion. Deflecting the power surge rushing between them, he backed off, and allowed her to give him a short grand tour of the condo.

He didn't miss the fact there were three bedrooms. "We need to christen each room."

"Not now, we don't. Now, we windsurf. Plus, I don't want to get used to having this all to myself. Mark and company will be arriving before we know it."

"What's luring him here?"

"A little something like his wedding. This place will be bursting at the seams this time next week — well, two weeks from Monday."

"Oh, yeah," TJ said." "I'm playing that gig at the Moana, right?"

"Correcto."

"Wanna be my date?"

"Can't. I'm standing up for Nikki, Maid of Honor," she

sang out, "and I don't know who my partner is."

"Um, Mel?" TJ cleared his throat, trying to look humble but surely failing. He puffed out his chest, feeling like a cuckoo attracting a mate. "That guy would be moi."

"Seriously? Get real."

"Honest. Mark asked me to stand up in the wedding for him. I can be your date."

"All righty then. Shall we go?"

TJ delayed their departure as he sang the lyrics to *Hat Check Girl* and danced Mellie around the living room. He ended their impromptu dance with a dip and another wet kiss.

He had to smile when Mellie ran her fingertips over her lips, grabbed her tote bag, and scooted out the door as if the building was on fire.

TJ followed with a satisfied grin.

The drive to Kailua beach was not far, but the view was breath-taking. They climbed, somewhat skirting Diamondhead. The view was a mixture of turquois, green, and blue ocean, which crashed against rocky shores, coating it with lacy white foam that sparkled in the sunlight.

When they reached the beach, there were a number of people there. Not as many as there were off Makena Pointe, but almost as many activities. Although, people were paddleboarding and snorkeling, most were windsurfing. It looked like everyone was having fun. Mellie's excitement was becoming infectious as she pulled him across the sand.

TJ was familiar with the shop on the beach that sold and rented equipment. It was where he'd bought his, and rental signs were posted nearby and in the windows. Boards of all sizes and types were lined up against one wall of the shop, each secured with a lock. They were bright, and some were incredibly detailed with wide swaths of color and intricate design. The sails were as different as each rider.

They chose a spot on the beach, and TJ unrolled the thin

bamboo mat he'd packed. He dropped his duffle bag on one corner, and Mellie set her tote bag on another.

He almost tripped over his tongue when Mellie removed her cover up. Her suit was a *Baywatch* red knock off, and the French cut emphasized her beautiful long legs. He couldn't wait to see her move in that suit. She'd give Pamela Anderson a run for her money. That much was for sure.

TJ covered her lush body with sunblock. Sometimes his hands lingered a bit longer than was necessary, deliberately, just to see the shivers run up and down her spine. Her skin felt like silk. They were both obviously experiencing tingles in all the right places. Right then, TJ wished the beach was empty where he could . . .

"Yoo-hoo. Earth to TJ, let's get this done. Do you realize you're just standing there drooling? While I'm flattered, I do want to get out there."

"Sorry about that. I was just mesmerized by your . . . uh . . . beauty."

"Booty, more likely." She grinned as she swatted him away.

TJ laid out the pieces of the rig. The sail, the jib line, the receptors, the fittings, and the board.

"Why is this thing in pieces?"

"If you want me to teach you to windsurf, this is what it takes. You need to know how to fit your rig. Before we do anything, let's get this on you." He gestured to a tight-fitting life jacket that matched her suit.

Over her protests that she could swim, he helped her put it on.

He carefully zipped it up over her full — *luscious* — chest, hoping not to catch her tender skin in the process.

"My rig, my rules." He somehow managed to stay calm yet firm. "Water safety is no joke. I wouldn't even bring you out here if I didn't know you were a strong swimmer. The boom

could swing and knock you out, you could drown in a heartbeat. Not gonna happen. Not on my watch." He donned his
own black, fitted life vest

"See, what's good for the goose," he said with a smirk, "is
good for the gander too. I could get bonked on the head as
easily as you."

Mellie was surprised when TJ insisted she do each step of
rigging the board. There was a lot to keep track of, and it
wasn't easy. He demonstrated and then undid his work to
have her try.

"I didn't realize this was so complicated," Mellie complained.

"Any good teacher would put you through these same
paces. Although I'm sure you could smile at any man, any
age, and he'd happily assemble this for you. But if you want
respect out here, you should be able to do this yourself."

Mellie was in for a surprise if she thought windsurfing was
going to be easy. She grumbled again when the day was half
over and they hadn't even gotten the rig into the water.

"Tell you what," he said. "It's going to take a solid week
before you'll be kitesurfing worthy. You've been patient and
willing to learn. Let's borrow my buddy's tandem board, and
we'll try to get you sailing." He pulled out his cell and called
his friend, Cody, who gave him his combination to his locker.
"I'll set this up, you do what you can, and then try to follow
my lead. You'll put your feet inside these foot holds. Think of
them as slip on sandals."

Once they got the two masts and sails attached and the
booms set up, TJ taught her how to read the wind, board the
rig and let the wind lift them. It took several unsuccessful at-
tempts before she correctly boarded.

TJ's control was tested when Mellie somehow managed to
fall off and get wet. TJ salivated. He caught his lip between
his teeth to keep himself from licking his chops.

It took a long time, but she finally was able to pull the sail up and hold onto the boom. Once she did, they soared across the waves. She tipped her sails and moved her feet until they were in the most unusual position ever known to windsurfing. Her soft body seemed Velcroed to his, the soft cheeks of her derriere plastered against his shaft.

He was turgid, but there was nothing he could do, as the sea held them captive now. *What I wouldn't give to whip it out and do right here, right now.* He wanted her badly. Fortunately, the wind was perfect, so their sail was nothing short of spectacular.

When the ride was over, Mellie looked shocked. "This takes a lot of upper body strength to not only lift the sail but also to hold the boom, shift my weight, and deal with the wind. I'm exhausted."

He laughed. "Told ya." TJ knew conditions were perfect for kite sailing." Do you mind if I go out for a bit and show you how it's done?"

"Be my guest," she said dropping a towel over her shoulders drying her dripping hair. "I'm happy to watch and learn."

Mellie was forced to admit she was impressed when TJ effortlessly boarded, hauled up the sail, grabbed the boom, and caught the wind in under ten seconds. It wasn't just his skill set, which to her eyes, looked exceptional. But he was also as fine a male specimen as she had ever seen.

He was tall, and the sun had streaked his hair as if he had had it highlighted professionally. His bathing suit sat low on his hips, showcasing his deep and even tan. He had the best set of man legs she had ever seen. He was Apollo, surfing with the wind blowing his hair behind, exposing a well featured face. His wide smile revealed white teeth, gorgeous against his tan face. He looked as comfortable on the sea as he had in bed. In short, he took her breath away.

She was in handsome hunk heaven.

Before the sun got too low in the sky, TJ sailed into shore. "Not fair to taunt the sharks. Twilight is prime time fishing here, and the sharks feed. I noticed schools of silver steel fish. They would make a tasty supper."

Mellie agreed and helped him dismantle and store the gear. When he began to unzip her life jacket, her breath caught in her throat as he inadvertently skimmed her breast with his knuckles.

"That was amazing," she breathed on a whisper.

"Yes. It was." He throatily agreed.

"No, the windsailing, silly. The high of that is unparalleled."

Looking deeply into her eyes he said, "It used to be the best high ever. But now, *you* are the biggest high I've ever known." He kissed her long and slow and thoroughly.

She pulled on her coverup and capris and joined him on the beautiful ride back, the wind blowing her hair free and wild, drying it. It was dark when they got back to Honolulu.

TJ took Mellie to *The Hat Check*, where they could feast. Maxine was in her element when she cooked for him. She discretely told him she was delighted to see him finally bring a date, and with a tender slap on his cheek, said *she will do*. TJ had never brought anyone else there before, so he wasn't totally surprised by Maxine's reaction.

Mellie ordered steamed crab over fettuccini Alfredo and a Pineapple-tini.

TJ ordered the same meal except he stuck with a cold Bud, which he chugged quickly.

Then with natural charm, no advance planning, and no

warning whatsoever for TJ, Mellie smiled at him.

Over a platter of steamed crab, Mellie gazed at him from under her long lashes, and TJ fell in love. Just like that. He hadn't planned on it. He just did it.

She cast her baby blues on him as she opened her crab legs and slowly slid the succulent meat into her mouth, hooking TJ in the process.

By dessert, she reeled him in.

He found himself caught for a lifetime and wasn't prepared for the sensual onslaught as their relationship seemed to catch fire and burned.

By the end of dinner, TJ was hungry for more than just good food. He was starved for Mellie. The long ride on his motor bike, the feel of their wet bare skin sliding together, and the close body contact while windsurfing, had all worked their magic. Add to that a shared passion for nature, sharks, and a budding relationship with kiteboarding, and it was enough to plunge him head over heels. He was frantic with need, begging for exquisite release.

When *The Sharks* played *Moon River*, TJ pulled Mellie into his arms. "There's next to no chances of me ever getting to dance, as I am the entertainment most of the time, so shall we dance, fair lady?" Once more he pulled her close until their bodies were so aligned nothing could come between them.'

Mellie's body melted into his.

He held her, swaying to the music, and breathing in the intoxicating scent of coconut in her hair.

TJ thought he should be in heaven with her in his arms. Yet he knew the slow burn he felt inside was going to ignite as if all hell were set loose if this went on much longer. He had to get her out of there, and to the nearest bed. That bed was in Mellie's condo. He didn't know how he was going to manage driving his bike when all he wanted was to do wild things with her right then and there.

Somehow, he made it to the Aloha Towers. Although he indulged in some passionate kissing and many well-placed caresses before the elevator doors opened, it was all he could manage not to go for it in the elevator. He had never had it this bad.

Eventually, he managed to get them into Mellie's condo.

They made it in the door before they were all over each other. Once inside, they started ripping their clothes off as fast as they could — TJ grabbing Mellie's as she grabbed his.

Naked, they tumbled to the floor, TJ hungrier than he had ever been for anyone. They were in a feeding frenzy of their own. No shark could beat in the hunger department. They each devoured every spot they could reach on the other's' body. Their love making was crazed, rolling in unparalleled ecstasy, entwined, completely captivated, until they climaxed together. They collapsed in a heap, sated and sleepy.

Sometime later, TJ pulled an afghan down from the settee, along with several pillows and covered them both. They slept where they were.

The chirp of TJ's cell awoke him with a start. There was no waking up slowly this time. The long, slow, relaxing but thrilling, weekend was over.

"Crap, I've got to be on Coconut Island this morning! I'm late! Gotta fly. Sorry." He planted a quick kiss somewhere on Mellie's head, pulled on his pants, and flew out the door.

Chapter Ten: Work

*G*ood morning to you too. Why, yes, I had a lovely time. Mellie blushed, remembering just how good a time she had had.

Mellie stayed busy with her usual schedule, including class work Mondays and Wednesdays with field work Tuesdays and Thursday. TJ stuck to his regular schedule as well, which consisted of computer work, writing his dissertation, field work gathering data, and working as a singer at *The Hat Check Lounge*.

Since it was Monday, she was studying and attending class, but she also needed to do something about a job. TJ had mentioned they were short-staffed at the Lounge. She made a note to ask him next time they went out.

Mellie smiled, thinking about how their schedules offered plenty of time for them to connect. The field work provided easy proximity and made the relationship just about perfect. There was no formal calling for a date. Things just flowed naturally from school to work, to the beach, and beyond. It was the most stress-free relationship she had ever had.

She sighed and concentrated on her studies. When she checked her email, she found one from Nikki, asking her to make a few arrangements.

To: Mellie Wheaton
From: Nikki
Subject: Operation bouquet check

Things are coming along well. I have a few requests, if you will be so kind. Say you will, and I won't have to kill you. I've ordered a wreath instead of a veil, and I have gardenias and lilies picked out for my bouquet. I ordered them from Petals at the Moana. Just make sure they are ready for delivery on Saturday July 19th at six p.m. at the hotel chapel.

Have you given thought to the harassment report? I was thinking if you are still obsessing, try journaling. It helps to write out what you experience. Many times, the answers are right there in your pen waiting for expression. I've attached pics of my dress – what do you think? Order a wreath for your headpiece, unless you've found something else. See you soon. XO, Nikki

To: Nikki
From: Mellie Wheaton
Subject: Operation Can Do
No problem. I had been thinking I could perch an emerald green Princess Kate hat on my head, but I think a Gardenia in my hair over my right ear will give you the look you're going for. Consider your wishes as my commands. I like the journal idea, but it might be full of TJ, the wedding singer. We're kind of a thing lately. You know him from Caren's wedding.
Xoxo
Mellie

TJ did not catch Mellie Monday afternoon as he had hoped, so he decided to do some windsurfing to ease the ache that thoughts of her created. The afternoon was windy enough for kiteboarding, but too strong for most surfers. Soon he was flying over the waves, caught up in a whirlwind of soaring sensation. He made some spectacular lifts that had people on shore pointing to him. He bucked the waves and hydroplaned across the water catching air while he tried aerial stunts that made him wish Mellie were there to see.

As if she had read his mind, he spied Mellie as she rode up on her motorbike and headed for shore.

"Hey, hot shot. Lookin' good out there," she greeted him, giving him a quick peck.

He wanted more than a taste, so he showed her a proper kiss. "I was just thinking about you, or rather trying not to think of you."

"And that's a good thing why?"

"Because I can't get you out of my mind. Makes it hard to work, survive, and thrive."

"Moi'?"

"Yes, you, Lady Godiva."

"That must mean you approve of this suit."

"And then some." He winked. "How about we do some windsurf lessons, since you're here?"

"Let's do."

Most of their lesson occurred near the shore, not on the water. Mellie protested her disappointment, but she complied with the rules. When they were finished, he treated her to a Mango Pango Shaved Ice Cone, the Hawaiian equivalent of a mainland snow cone only much better because it was made with island fruit juices.

"TJ?"

"Yes."

"You don't know the question yet, be serious."

"I am serious. This is me being serious. What can I do for you?"

"Get me hired." Mellie looked at him grinning.

"You aren't ready to give kiteboarding lessons yet," he teased. "Anything else I can do for you? Like satisfy that craving for a certain kitesurfer extraordinaire, for example?"

She laughed. "I need a job. Know of any?"

"Maybe. What can you do?"

"Sing for my supper like you do?"

"Tips for that are better if you waitress, too. How about you start with that?"

"You might be sorry . . ." she stated, "But I'm game."

"I'll talk to both my band and Sam, the owner. Come by during my break and I'll introduce you. You'll have to audition for the boys. I'll talk to them. Maybe we can build you into the set."

"Deal."

They shook on it.

After dinner, Mellie motored over to check out *The Hat Check Lounge* hoping she'd get a job. She wore a very short stylish black skirt and a low-cut white tank. She hoped she looked like a waitress but wished she had chosen a strapless sequined top instead. She was sure she was a better singer.

TJ and the band quit for the break. Several bandmates waved at her approvingly. And was that Burt Raines-Forest who wolf whistled his greeting? It was.

"You didn't tell me Burt was part of the *Sharks*."

TJ merely shrugged. "The subject didn't come up. Sam, this is the girl I was telling you about. Mellie Wheaton, Mark Wheaton's kid sister."

Sam took one look at her and smiled. "You're hired."

At any other time, Mellie would have been fuming at being treated like a sex object, but she desperately needed work, and they'd soon find out what she could and could not do.

She was learning when and where to pick her feminist battles. At the moment, she felt dreamy and good. She wasn't looking for troubles or issues. No causes tonight. Tonight was all about getting a job.

On the other hand, she thought the waitress *uniform* from the forties was cute and fit the theme of the place. She already had plans for how she would wear her hair in a 40s hair do.

"When can I start?"

"How about tonight?" Sam said, handing her an apron he grabbed from Maxine.

Maxine paired her with a girl named Kate, who Mellie had seen on campus.

Kate sized her up and said, "Bend over when you serve the men and you'll get great tips.

"Thanks," Mellie returned. "I think."

She tied the small back apron around her waist and went to table 5, where two men openly ogled her. She was uncomfortable, but she took their orders. She got the order for grilled mahi right, but apparently no one had ordered a hamburger, rare, with Swiss cheese. Fortunately, the man didn't complain. Not too loudly, anyway. In her haste to return the food, she knocked over the pitcher of beer that was on Kate's tray, which soaked both her and her client's clothes.

She looked up to see that TJ noticed and cringed.

Mellie picked up some cocktail napkins, and in a flurry, tried to mop the mess off Kate's chest.

Wisely, she left the male patron's wet lap alone, although he waved her over to try. She passed on that opportunity. She didn't make much by the time those costs were taken from her tips. But she had a job, and she'd get to see more of TJ.

TJ must have noticed her slumped shoulders and heard her sigh. He shook his head and shrugged. "Lighten up. This is your first night. Chillax. You'll get the hang of it."

But she didn't.

Unfortunately, that was only the beginning of a very long night. *The Hat Check Lounge* closed at 2:00 a.m., and Mellie was exhausted and upset with herself.

At last her shift was over. Discouraged, she deposited her apron in the laundry bin after removing her meager tips. She left.

The full moon lit her way back to the condo.

The next day, TJ was glad they were having a later-than-usual start that morning. He had divided the tasks among the teams. This trip they were baiting the water with shrimp hoping to lure the sharks toward the *Meyers Research Ship.*

The crew were anchored in an open area of sea, where people didn't normally fish, swim, or snorkel. TJ distributed the bait while Mellie counted whatever came their way. Her body was a golden paradise he never grew tired of watching. When there were no sharks in view, there was always Mellie. For now, at least.

TJ felt the two of them were settling into a comfortable relationship. Since they were now intimate, it was much easier following the *no on sea, yes on land* policy. The tension close proximity created now had a relief valve, making things smoother when they worked together. Like many young lovers, TJ's world was shrinking to just the two of them.

The windsurfing lessons had, so far, consisted of learning terms, assembling the rig, and learning wind and balance theory, so there was plenty of time to indulge in heavy kissing and earth-shaking sex. They had, as TJ had predicted, christened every room in Mark's condo. They made love everywhere. Nothing was off limits. They had even indulged out on the lanai.

TJ smiled at the memory of Mellie sitting in the well of the wicker chair, legs open as he stood before her. If anyone had thought to look, they'd have just seen his butt but nothing much of Mellie. With the possibility of being seen, they had made it a quickie, but their climax was as strong as ever.

He shook his head to clear the memory. It was time to get back to work.

Each night Mellie waitressed was almost worse than the preceding one. She constantly had miscalled orders, spilt drinks, dumped food in a lap and dropped and broke dishes.

She was often in tears. Especially when she saw TJ cringe each time she messed up.

For Mellie, the best part of working at *The Hat Check* was when TJ and his band started playing songs she knew. She would sing along, out loud and clear. It always helped ease her frustrations.

That night, Sam called her over. "Hey kid. It's obvious you are no waitress."

Mellie's eyes started to fill with tear. *Oh, no. I can't lose this job.*

"But," he continued, "you can sing. So sing. No more waitressing."

Mellie shucked her apron. Finally, she was getting to do all singing and no waitressing. No doubt everyone was happy about the change.

After work, Mellie was standing on her lanai with TJ, looking out at the ocean. TJ mentioned that the weekend was coming up and wondered what they were going to do.

"I know what you do for work and school, but what do you do for fun?" he asked.

"I thought it was going to be windsurfing, but since I'm still in learning mode, mostly on shore, I can't say that. I haven't had a chance to see much of the island. I know Kauai some because Caren and Chance held their wedding there. We spent a few weeks doing things together, getting to know each other while Nikki and Mark were busy being wedding planners. I'd like to paddleboard, but my real passion seems to be exploring beaches. I want to see every beach and paddleboard wherever I can."

"I can help make that happen." TJ came and stood behind her as they watched the rolling surf crash into the golden beach beneath the towering green Koala Mountains. "You saw some of the island when we went to the ranch snipe hunting. You know what? We ought to go to Pearl Beach. It's close to the naval base. We can watch the submarine races. There's plenty to explore there." He waggled his eyebrows and leered.

Mellie leaned into him, laughing "Right. As if. Not happening."

"You have complaints about our first date?"

"That was a date?"

"Dates with me are so easy that you don't even know you're on one."

"I guess. We did have dinner."

"*The Hat Check's* food is way good. Now that you work there, you'll get all the food you can eat, so you can pay up your debt."

"Debt?" She lifted an eyebrow, questioningly.

"The Menehune," he reminded. "The Hawaiian leprechaun? I presume you googled it?"

"There was a race of little people who were said to complete wondrous mechanical engineering feats by night, but I'm not sure you'd call them leprechauns."

"They worked magic, yes? Close enough," TJ announced and smiled." You owe me dinner."

"I think that can be arranged. How do you like the food at *The Hat Check Lounge*? That I can afford."

"How about we spend Saturday at Ala Moana Beach and do some paddleboarding? Then let *The Hat Check Lounge* feed us?"

"It's a date." She smiled. "You're on."

TJ thoughts seemed to be more Mellie-filled than shark-filled lately. He could not keep the images of her stunning figure and golden skin out of his mind. It was easy to remember the red-hot passion that licked his loins when they were together making love. Even when they couldn't connect, her very nearness thrilled him to his core and made his blood run hot. He had never met anyone like her.

She shared his passion for the sea, and sex in the sea was an unparalleled experience for him. He'd had been working on a song for her that he hoped to sing to her soon. *Hot Legs. Hot lips. Hot from her fingertips to her hips. Hot. Hot. Hot. The lady is hot and hot for me.* That was a wrap. He was beginning to fall and fall hard for her. *Is she falling, too?*

Mellie transferred some of the skills she was learning from windsurfing and applied them to her paddle-boarding, which improved and became fun. She had done some in Kauai and had to laugh when she recalled Nikki's inability to master the sport.

Come to think of it, Nikki's skills weren't of the physical kind, and her concern for Mellie's well-being couldn't be disputed. The journaling idea had been right on. Writing out what she thought and felt about Wolfe was liberating. She was beginning to heal. Her newfound relationship with TJ was heaven sent and helped even more.

Nikki's last email included several photos of her and Mark's wedding in Detroit. The Matthews—Chance, and Nikki's sister, Caren—were present there. From the pictures, it looked like a fabulous and elegant affair. If memory served her, Mark and Nikki used the traditional vows, eliminating the *obey* clause.

The ceremony had been held in the Old St Mary's Church in Greek Town in Detroit. It was a twilight ceremony complete with candles fastened at each pew. Nikki wore her hair in an up-do with a few soft curls running down her cheeks, the same way she had worn it for Caren's wedding.

Nikki's dress was ivory silk with a deep Sweetheart neckline. Her veil was finger-tip length with an intermittent sprinkling of sequins. Mellie knew Nikki chose that particular veil because Mark had loved that look on her. The top of the gown was also ablaze in sequins, but the bottom was pure satin. The gown was a simple but elegant A line, which flattered Nikki's generous curves. The remarkable thing was that Mark had designed the dress. *Who knew he ran that deep? Guess he really got into wedding planning after all.*

Mark and Nikki's story was iconic. Both had been forced by circumstances into becoming co-wedding planners for Caren and Chance Matthews, and now they were planning their own ceremonies.

Because Mark had his heart set on a beach wedding, two ceremonies made sense. He loved the romance, the sunsets, and the lush tropical beauty of the islands themselves.

Nikki wrote she felt she deserved two ceremonies since she had waited so long to meet the right guy.

Mellie smiled to herself, thinking of how well the two of them meshed after a rocky beginning. When Nikki and Mark arrived, Mellie planned to get all the details, right down to the wedding night.

CHAPTER ELEVEN: THE FAM

Mid-term break arrived, and Mellie took advantage while TJ continued with his research. When she wasn't in class, she practiced windsurfing whenever she could. There were always plenty of people willing to help, and she was getting fairly good at it—much to TJ's delight.

She loved the view of Oahu from the water and enjoyed sailing free as a bird beneath with sun caressing her skin and the trade winds lifting her hair. The scent of salt in the air served as an exotic perfume known only on the ocean. The sea was beautiful and satisfying. She never ceased to be moved by joining with the sea, surf, and sky.

Mellie was relaxing in Mark's condo, taking a bath, soaking the stresses and strains of the day away. She knew TJ would join her soon. Lately they had fallen into a routine of sorts. TJ finished work later than she did. She had no sound equipment to deal with like he did. She sang for her supper, then headed home after her last set.

She had given TJ a key, so she wasn't surprised when she heard him enter the condo.

"In here," she sang out from the bathroom.

"You descent?"

"Hardly."

TJ was there in a heartbeat, shedding his clothes as fast as he could, then climbed into the bathtub. Mark had spared no expense when he'd had the condo built. The Jacuzzi tub could easily accommodate them both.

TJ wasted no time, caressing every inch of her body using

his hands in place of a loofa. It didn't take much before they were deeply involved with kissing and passionate lovemaking.

Mellie lay in his arms as he cleansed every place she had. He was in the process of milking another soul-shaking climax from her overly sensitive center when she screamed her release. It surprised them both, but not as much as hearing someone coming through the door of the condo.

Mellie scrambled out of the tub looking for a towel, which were in short supply. The bubbles in the Jacuzzi were long gone as well. *What the hell! What's happening?*

She heard voices and realized the entire family had piled into the living room.

Mark's worst fear had come true. His kid sister was in big trouble. Bad trouble. Screaming trouble. He ran in the direction of the screams. He should never have allowed her to stay here alone. She should be in a dorm. Things like this didn't happen in dorm rooms. Did they? He didn't know. He didn't care. This was about to stop.

He barged into the bathroom. "What the fuck!" he yelled, grabbing TJ by the throat, ready to punch him out.

TJ sputtered, trying to disengage and stand up, but he slipped and banged his knee hard against the side of the tub yelling, "Ow!"

Mellie let out a yelp and screamed, grabbing the only covering available, a washcloth. She tried — though failing — to cover herself. "You, Neanderthal. What do you think you're doing?"

"I'm protecting you," Mark yelled. "What's it look like?"

A dripping TJ was hobbling around clutching his injured knee to his chest when Mark hauled off and clocked him.

TJ went down for the count. *Ha! Mark, one, TJ, out cold.*

"That's my *boyfriend*," Mellie cried.

"Now, now," Grandma Daisy said. She found a towel and tossed it to Mellie.

Mellie wrapped it around herself, still spluttering angrily.

"Everyone just settle down," Grandpa Gus commanded.

"Get out!" Mellie shouted, "All of you."

"What . . . I live here, ya know." Mark glared at his sister, both shocked and surprised. "Didn't you get my text? We're *supposed* to be here."

"What text?"

"Never mind. I told you we'd be here at eighteen hundred hours and here we are. Obviously, you didn't get it. Other things must have been on your mind." Mark walked around somewhat dazed. He shook his head to clear it, then shook his swelling fist. "Son of a bitch." He followed that with a whole host of other expletives, which Daisy had never heard before, judging from the look on her face.

"You've done enough damage for one night," Mellie shouted. "The least you can do is help him."

"We need ice," Gus said.

Daisy disappeared, then returned with some ice, a frozen bag of peas, and some steak. It was clear that TJ was going to have a shiner come morning.

"Help me get him off of this wet floor, you big baboon," Mellie ordered. "You could have killed him. What if he had hit his head?"

Mark complied and got TJ off the floor and onto the couch, throwing a pillow over the man's lap.

Daisy applied the ice to TJ's head, the peas to his knee, and the steak to his rapidly reddening eye.

"What about me?" Mark complained. "Some thanks I get for saving you. Besides, my knuckles hurt."

"You're lucky that's all that hurts."

"Well, my pride is suffering too, but hey . . ."

Mellie just looked at him clearly exasperated. "Get over yourself."

"Look, I'm sorry I went into b*ig brother* mode. I heard you scream out and — "

"Coming! Not that it's any of your business, I was coming." Mellie's voice rising another octave. "Ever hear of that?"

"Holy shit. Wait. That was . . . Hell on a horse!" Mark felt his face heating up. "I need a drink."

"He's heard that all right," Nikki said. "We all did, but he still has a long, long way to go before I get him civilized. Then I'll work on the *becoming a grown-up*. But first things first."

"I need a drink," he repeated, then headed for the fridge and pulled out a Sam Adams. Sighing loudly, he went out on the liana, sank into a chair, stretched out his legs, and took a long pull on his beer while listening to Nikki and Mellie commiserated on all things male.

"Here's one thing you must remember, Mellie" Nikki said "Men—all of them—are assholes. And when you forget, they'll remind you. By the way, TJ is waking up."

"Fuck a duck!" TJ groaned. "He hit me."

"More like knocked you out cold," Mellie remarked." Just saying."

"I don't think you should drive home. Not after a blow to the head," Nikki noted. "Someone will have to keep an eye on him. Wake him up every few hours."

"That would be moi. Don't worry about him," Mellie said. "I'll take care of him."

Mark turned around in time to see Mellie leading TJ to her room, her glare just daring him to interfere with the sleeping arrangements.

Chapter Twelve: Wedding Plans

Mellie entered her bedroom with a fresh ice pack. TJ had woken with the mother of all headaches and a black eye to match. She smiled at him and handed over the ice.

TJ sat on the edge of the bed, holding the pack to his swollen eye. "Coulda been worse," he muttered.

"How?" Mellie asked.

"I could have had a real hangover. After the punch in the eye, I just *feel* like I have one."

"Poor baby," Mellie crooned. "Here, let me make it all better."

She leaned in to kiss his brow, resting her weight on him.

He yelped. "Bad knee!"

Mellie leaped to her feet backing away. "Sorry. Just trying to kiss and make it all better."

After a few minutes, she helped him out to the kitchen, where Daisy was whirling around, preparing breakfast. The condo Mellie had once perceived as spacious now seemed to team with people, wandering around in a jet lagged, too-full late-night daze. Yet Daisy, Gus, and Nikki somehow kept from running into each other.

Nikki handed Mellie a cup of freshly brewed Kona coffee. Both Nikki and her sister, Caren, had fallen in love with Hawaii's home-grown brew when they were planning Caren's wedding to Chance.

"Nothing like a fresh cup of Joe," Gus said, intercepting the mug on the way to Mellie's hand.

Mellie grinned and patted him lovingly on the shoulder.

Daisy and Gus had taken up the role of parents for the whole group. While she and Mark were new additions, it resembled a made-for-TV instant family. Their lives were totally entwined, with everyone benefiting.

Nikki pressed another mug into her hands. "You up for some wedding work?"

"Yup."

"Drink up. We have a site to check out. Flowers to fix. Hair to do."

"Music to arrange? I hope," TJ asked.

Mark entered the cacophony of chatter in the kitchen. He gave Nikki a quick kiss and Mellie a hug, then he approached his friend.

He stretched out his arm and shook his hand as he nudged TJ. "Sorry about that, dude. Kid sister and all . . . But seriously, I am sorry."

"It's all good," TJ said, waving the Hawaiian shaka sign. "Hang loose and all that."

"Come with me." Mark tilted his head, taking TJ off to the side, away from the others.

Mark leaned in and kept his voice low. "If you come close to hurting her like that shit Wolfe, I will nail your knees to your surfboard."

"Good to know," TJ responded, looking serious as a heart attack. "But I won't hurt her. I haven't told her yet, but I'm in this for the long haul. I love her, man."

That surprised him, but he kept his expression neutral. "Then we're clear?"

"Yeah, brah. We're cool."

Mark slapped TJ on the back and noticed his friend's wince, so he helped him back to his seat at the counter.

Mellie helped Daisy hand out breakfast plates to everyone. The women concentrated on all things wedding at the kitchen island center while the guys headed for the lanai.

By time Mellie and the girls finished breakfast, they'd made plans for the afternoon and were all set to seize the day.

"I brought the CD from our ceremony in Detroit. We can watch it this evening." Nikki set the disc atop the DVR. "Now, let's roll."

"We don't have to worry about the music, really, because TJ does that for a living," Mellie said. "He knows to at least play *Hat Check Girl, Blue Moon, Blue Bayou, Cheek to Cheek,* and *I Only Have Eyes for You.* I am singing with him, so if you don't mind, I'll be part of that."

"Perfect," Nikki said giving her a squeeze as they headed out. "And don't worry. They have Gus, so he'll make things go as they should. He'll keep things under control."

"Hm," Nikki added. "Three men planning together. What could go wrong? That's downright scary."

"Let's start out at the Chapel at the Moana," Daisy suggested. "I want to make sure they are ready for us, and I haven't really seen the venue, either."

"I haven't either," Mellie said, "I've seen the hotel, but not the chapel or the Rooftop Renaissance Garden Room."

"Then you are both in for a treat," Nikki promised. "The chapel is at the very top of the hotel, and once you exit the chapel you enter rooftop heaven. It'll be an open-air trip to paradise."

"Wait. I thought *that* didn't happen until everything is all over," Mellie quipped.

It was a very short walk to the *Moana.* A moment later, they entered the chapel, which had a full ocean panoramic view from all sides. They released their breath in one collective sigh at the incredible beauty spread out before them. The Pacific rolled in all its aqua, sapphire, and turquoise splendor

"Why," Daisy gasped, "it doesn't need a thing. No tulle, no ribbons, no flowers. It's perfect. Our job here is finished. All that's missing is you and Mark. I don't know what more you can bring to it. The setting is God-perfect. Leave it as it is."

Mellie had to agree. "The chapel view does take your breath away. It's the perfect place to begin a new life together. God, nature, and the man you love," she sighed. "So much for my flowers."

"What flowers?" Nikki demanded. "All I asked for was gardenias and lilies in my bouquet. And a matching wreath."

"Wellll, call me a romantic, but I did order a few pink roses as a carryover from your bouquet in Detroit," Mellie admitted, feel the heat rise in her cheeks.

"What else?" Nikki prodded. "Spill it."

"And a baby pink rosebud with mini gardenia for Mark's boutonniere."

"Okay, I can live with that," Nikki said cautiously, "but nothing else. I mean it."

"God's truth." Mellie claimed, raising her right hand like she was about to swear in at court on the Bible. "Nothing else. Not even a fern. Well . . . Maybe, a fern or two."

"Hmm, ferns are overrated, but I can handle that. Just don't want a whole lot of fussy stuff like tulle bows, candles on the aisle, flowers in overload."

Their mission completed, Mellie led the ladies to an enjoyable lunch at *The Banyan* overlooking the sapphire ocean topped with white waves undulating across the sea languidly, easily, slowly.

After lunch, they checked out the Rooftop Renaissance Garden Room on the 6th floor in the historic section of the hotel, which had an earthshaking full ocean view, where nary a fern was found. Not even Nikki could fault the perfection of the venue.

They returned to the condo to change into their swimsuits. Mellie took a moment to admire her new natural weave bikini adorned with tiny seashells and fringe in the mirror hanging on the bathroom door. She smiled and wondered what TJ would think of it, then followed the others down to collapse on the beach.

As they sipped island concoctions, they discussed more wedding details. Their drinks were served by a handsome young stud who nearly dropped their drinks as he gawked at Mellie. Mellie nursed a Tropical Itch, and Nikki sucked on a Hawaiian Shirley Temple. Daisy had shocked them all when she ordered a smoking Blue Hawaii.

The discussion turned to the dresses Mellie and Daisy were going to wear for the wedding. Nikki reminded Mellie that she was to wear the green one she worn at Caren's wedding, and Daisy chuckled as she admitted she would be wearing the same dress she wore to Caren's ceremony, too.

"I've never been able to get much use out of wedding wear until I came into this family." Daisy laughed." Seems like I've been to three, including my own. I do love weddings."

They lounged in the sun for a while longer, then left the beach for the condo. When they got there, Mark and Gus were grilling fresh marinated mahi-mahi. Mellie poked holes in the potatoes to nuke them while Daisy put a salad together. They ate around the table each reciting a list of things done for the wedding. Then they moved to the living room, where a 65-inch flat screen rested above a natural stone fireplace that was very modern. Mark flicked the switch and the thin gas jets came on creating a nice ambiance.

Nikki put their wedding CD into the player and sat back. Everyone watched in shared joy as she—a vision in her gown if she did say so—posed with Mark, resplendent in his grey morning suit with a striped coral tie. She closed her eyes, re-living the day in her mind as they all watched the video.

Chance escorted Caren down the candlelit aisle, following Emily as she tossed flower petals from her basket. Caren and Emily were wearing matching satin dresses that had graceful tiers of ruffles flowing down the light salmon concoctions.

Everyone watching choked up when Benjamin, their adopted ten-year-old son, dressed in a tuxedo matching Mark's, walked down the aisle with a pillow bearing the rings. Once they were all in place, both Gus and Daisy led Nikki down the rose petal strewn aisle. The organ played, the choir sang, and Gus placed Nikki's hand in Mark's.

When the question *Who gives this bride in matrimony?* was asked, and Daisy and Gus responded proudly but in a choked voice said in unison, *We do*, there wasn't a dry eye in the house.

Mark slipped the two-carat, cushion cut diamond ring, with a pearl set on both sides, onto her finger and made her his for all time.

In a whirlwind of emotion, Mark led her down the aisle and whisked her away in a carriage to Belle Isle's Scott fountain. Colored lights lit up the monument as they posed for pictures in front of it. Then the rode in a chauffeured classic car to *The Whitney* for a very elaborate and elegant reception.

Their meal was sit down. White linen covered the tables, while the chairs had pale rose covers that matched the roses Nicki carried as she made her way down the aisle. Crystal vases, very clear and very tall, held matching long stem pink roses. The tall vases gave the guests seated at round tables a clear view of all the festivities. When it came time to throw the bouquet, no one dared bring a catcher's mitt like she had done at Caren's reception.

When the video was over, the family watching with Nikki

were all in tears. Everyone cleared their throats and wiped their eyes, appearing somewhat embarrassed by their response.

Mellie wiped her eyes. "OMG. That was way cray-cray. How are we going to top that?"

"How 'bout those vows?" Mark puffed his chest out. "All I had to do was to say I'd love, cherish and obey." He winked.

"Ahem, everyone," Nikki said. "Please note, I did *not* say obey."

"My fav part was when Benjamin lit his candle from both of yours when you lit the Unity Candle." Mellie walked over to Mark and gave him a kiss on the cheek. "Am I right or am I right? That was your doing?"

"He's my boy," Mark said with a glint of tears in his eyes. "But when Ben said *I do too* after Nikki said her vows, I thought I'd just pass out."

"That was amazing," Nikki agreed. "I have everything I never knew I wanted. And what's more, I'm doing it all again tomorrow. What was I thinking?"

"I'm thinking I better get you over to the penthouse at the Moana. Go get your things, Mrs. Wheaton," Mark said as he urged her to her feet. "Remember, it was your idea not to spend the night together before our second wedding."

Then he plastered her with a prolonged, lingering kiss.

"Why did I do that?" Nikki cried, tearing herself free. "That was damn dumb."

"Two words," Mark said in return, *"Penthouse, Moana."*

She laughed. "Now I recall." She laughed.

"Your new wedding dress was sent over earlier," Mark said. "I delivered it myself, and before you go any farther, I did not peek at it. Though I did design it, remember?"

"How could I forget?" Nikki said and laughed. "I told you so. You were a born wedding planner. Most of the details in this venue are Mark's idea."

Making their goodbyes, Mark grabbed the luggage Nikki needed for the night, and they made the short walk to the Moana, with the flicker of the tiki torches lighting the way. The royal palms greeted them as they entered the stately historic hotel known as the White House of the Pacific. They passed through the white wide foyer of the hotel and went directly to the penthouse.

The view was spectacular even by night. The tiki torches lit the grounds and beach as the Pacific gently rolled into shore. White foam that looked like white lace topped each and every wave.

Just inside the doorway, Mark took her into his arms. "By this time tomorrow, you'll be my *first lady* for the day and all the tomorrows to come."

He kissed her sweetly, and Nikki clung to him breathlessly.

"Change your mind?" he teased.

"No way, big guy." She moved out of his arms, reluctantly but firmly. "We're doing this right. Go."

Mark threw her his most charming boyish grin, "You sure? A quickie for luck? To tide you over? After all, we're already married."

"Out." She marched him to the door and closed it firmly, sliding the lock into place.

"Killjoy," he called out.

"You'll thank me in the morning."

"You'll be sorry."

"Nighty-night. Buh-bye," she called through the door.

Nikki turned to face the room, and true to his word, her gown hung in the closet, covered by its protective bag.

CHAPTER THIRTEEN: THE SECOND WEDDING

TJ woke early, and the games began. He was busy with *the Sharks* getting their equipment over to the roof top venue at the Moana.

The University of Hawaii was holding its annual Marine Mania meeting in the ballroom next to the chapel. TJ had to attend that function, so he had a tape prepared for his break when he would join his team for a short *meet-and-greet* and then return to finish the gig for the wedding. He'd have to time things just right to get it all to work. *It's all good.* He had to keep a clear head so it all would go as planned without a hitch. *Good thing my wedding duds will work for the huge fish fry.*

Nikki had an attack of nerves, but the flurry of wedding prep made time fly. Before too long, Mellie and Daisy finally arrived at the Moana to help her into the gown that Mark had designed specifically for this wedding. She was grateful for the help.

Daisy eased the long white gown with its low square neckline over Nikki's hair, careful not to muss it. She had insisted Nikki wrap her updo in swathes of toilet paper to preserve its shape. Nikki looked like she was wearing a turban, but had to admit it did preserve her hairdo.

Mellie tried to pull the dress, festooned with tiny sequined starfish, down over the full swell of Nikki's breasts, but there wasn't much top to pull down.

Nikki had to smile. *Mark purposely designed it low to empha-size my curves. That rascal.*

"I love how Mark put a heart-shaped cutout on the back," Mellie said.

Daisy delicately moved Mellie out of the way as she smoothed the back of the gown. "The cap sleeves are delight-ful. They remind me of Caren's dress."

"Mark was over the top when he ruched the bodice," Mellie observed. "You could see what his mind was on."

"That's my man, all right," Nikki agreed.

She watched in the mirror as Mellie and Daisy lifted and placed the delicate wreath onto her head. The baby pink roses worked well with her auburn hair. She wore her mother's sin-gle-strand pearls, and topped the whole look off with the matching pearl earrings and bracelet that Mark had given her on their first wedding day a week earlier. She had to admit she looked stunning, glowing with a joy and natural beauty that was hers alone. She was ready.

Daisy and Mellie handed her the bouquet of tropical lilies and gardenia — with a few pink roses — and they went up to the chapel.

The chapel, while small, was brimming with their friends and some of Mark's business acquaintances.

This time it was Gus alone who escorted Nikki down the aisle, while TJ escorted Mellie and Burt Raines-Forest did the honors with Daisy. This was going to be a much simpler cer-emony, but every bit as meaningful.

Again, Nikki was overcome by the view of the rolling Pa-cific, but when she reached the altar there was no Mark. *Where is he?*

Kekoa was standing in as their kahuna because Kahuna Kane's baby chose that day to arrive. He looked around ex-pectantly, obviously seeking but not finding Mark.

Nikki shifted uncomfortably. *WTF? Where is he already?*

"Look," Daisy whispered, pointing to her husband. "This isn't like Mark. Gus was part of the plan and has kept an eye on things, and he doesn't look at all concerned. Everything must be okay."

Kekoa didn't skip a beat and set the tone of the ceremony with a huge, rousing "Aloha!"

The guests gave an enthusiastic *Aloha!* greeting in return.

"We gather together, again, to unite these two—dis *one* fo' now—in wedlock. Trust me, Nikki not so sure 'bout all dis marriage business, and Mark, he not much betta."

People chuckled while Nikki acknowledged her hesitations. She had been old enough to appreciate the less than idyllic marriage of her parents and had fully intended to remain single until the magic of Mark took her to these uncharted but beautiful shores.

Suddenly a roar filled the air, and everyone turned as one when the helicopter swooped to land on the helipad outside like an action movie. Then Mark, handsome in his tux, exited the craft and calmly took his place beside her.

A collective gasp resounded despite the loud roaring of the copter, then laughter erupted. Even Nikki laughed.

"Talk about an arrival," TJ said. "We'll be talking about this forever."

Nikki punched, then slapped Mark on the shoulder. "You're not supposed to upstage the bride." She kept her tone low, but the humor of the situation was not lost on her.

Mark obviously had planned this as well.

Gus looked pretty pleased with himself.

"What?" Mark asked. "It's the second time around. We needed some drama."

"I'll give you drama," Nikki pledged, hitting him again this time with her bouquet.

As if Mark's entrance wasn't enough excitement, when

time came for the vows, the whole thing broke down.

As Mark turned to Nikki, he took her hands and began to recite his vows. Nikki in her no-nonsense way took charge.

With a smirk, she interrupted. "I know the drill. Yadda, yadda, yadda, do you?"

"Yadda, I do." Mark said

"Yadda, me too. Is this enough drama for you?"

They laughed as they were joyously pronounced man and wife.

Mark kissed Nikki enthusiastically, and they headed off to their roof-top reception.

Everyone was laughing, teasing, and talking up a storm.

TJ got the music going.

The food was exceptional. The caterer, Kanani, set up the pepper-encrusted roast pork station while grilled mahi-mahi plates and lomi-lomi salmon were served with fingerlings potatoes and braised asparagus.

The cake was a wonderous confection that resembled nothing Nikki had ever seen anywhere. It was made of three wavy layers and frosted using all the unique colors of the Pacific. It was breath-taking and magnificent. The glory of the gently curling ceaseless waves of the Pacific were captured in cake and icing to perfection. The bride and groom atop the masterpiece were riding on a tandem paddleboard.

"That had to be custom-made. Look, the bride is sitting, the groom paddling," Daisy said.

Nikki laughed along with Daisy. Those who knew her well knew she had no sense of balance.

Overall, the wedding was nothing short of a full-on blast.

Mark was lost in a world consisting of just Nikki and himself. He was torn from it to have wedding pictures taken and to cut the wedding cake. Then he rejoined the festivities partying mightily on a natural high.

Once those were done, Mark whispered in Nicki's ear and they left. Mark led the way a section of the veranda where a paved path led to the ocean. There in the moonlight, he removed his lei and carefully placed it around her, kissing her deeply. He had told her he had wanted a beachside service, and now they were having it. He knew she fretted about her dress. He took steps to ensure she had worried for nothing. The spot he had selected was private and beautiful. Only moonlight touched her dress.

"Satisfied now?" he asked.

She giggled, noticing the cleared path beneath her feet.

He put a hand to his ear. The sound of the music drifted to them." May I have the honor of the next dance?" There they danced under the moonlight and stars, the fairy lights twinkling in the tropical greenery.

He led her by the hand to return to the reception amid hoots, hollers, and catcalls about *quickies*.

Mellie left the roof top terrace, needing to use the ladies room, which was shared by the ballroom where a banquet was being held. If her memory was accurate, TJ had to make an appearance there as well. She spied him just inside, so she ducked in to snatch a kiss, then she froze on the spot. There stood a young John Kennedy look alike. Only one man in her experience looked and stood as if the world were made just for him. It was Wolfe Wunderlik.

"Well, well, well" he drawled, raising a concise and well-practiced eyebrow. "Look who we have here. Fancy meeting you here."

"What the hell are you doing here, Wolfe?" Mellie demanded.

"I could ask you the same thing," he replied in his smooth tone.

There was something that went beyond body and soul when it came to Wolfe and her. She had never felt such a compelling draw before or since. What she had with TJ was far and away better, but she could not—even now—shed herself of that mysterious, inexplicable *something* that drew her in like a moth to a flame. It was that certain, and that deadly.

She knew better now, though. She was not the same starry-eyed girl blown away by his attention and good looks. Power and prestige were seductive. But that was over.

She looked toward TJ, who smiled when they made eye contact.

TJ wasn't blind. Mellie's stance spoke volumes. Something was way wrong. She was standing stiff as a board, and she was pale beneath her tan. Senses on full alert, his protective mode homed in on her like a heat-seeking missile. He was beside her in seconds.

He looked her over quickly. "Everything all right here?"

Mellie mumbled something to the effect that she was fine, but any fool could see she wasn't.

He could swear she was trembling. He moved in closely.

"Dr. Wolfe Wunderlik," the man standing next to Mellie said, extending his hand. "Mellie, dear, why don't you introduce me to your, ah, little friend here?"

"Huh?" TJ muttered.

"Fine. Have it your way," Mellie said coolly. "Wolfe, TJ. TJ, Wolfe."

"You're Wolfe?" TJ said, catching on. *What the hell?*

Wolfe merely nodded in acknowledgment, a small, satisfied smile crossed his handsome, even features.

"This isn't over," TJ promised. "But unfortunately, we

can't settle this here. Look Mellie, I have to do this *frickin' meet and frickin' greet* thing. As soon as I can, I'll catch you at the wedding. You okay?"

Mellie assured him again.

Reluctantly, TJ walked away. "Later."

Mellie turned on her heels to leave the banquet room when she found Wolfe at her side.

He took her arm and led her out.

"I mean it, Wolfe, stay the hell away from me."

"You can do better than that. What kind of greeting is this? Don't be like that," he said. "It's unbecoming and drawing attention."

"How am I supposed to be?" she asked bitterly, "All warm and fuzzy? Maybe I should ask after Monique. How rude of me. How is she by the way?"

"Look, Monique was a mistake. Pure and simple. End of story. But I'm here now, and so are you. This is the isle of love, and we could be better occupied."

"Don't even go there with me. Don't even. What are you doing here, anyway?"

"Well darling, don't you pay attention in class? I'm tonight's keynote speaker, but enough about me. Why are you here?"

"I'm standing up in my brother's wedding, not that it matters to you."

"You're wrong about that. Everything about you concerns me." He made a move toward the wedding reception, smiled at her, and looked over his shoulder. "That could have been you and I saying *I do*, you know."

She gaped, sure that her jaw hit the floor with her shock. "Whatever."

"We'll see each other shortly. I'll be taking over the second half of Dr. Roland's course. You're in that class, yes? His research is heating up, and I'm taking over for him as guest lecturer. Look, I really would like to continue this discussion. I can see we have a lot to talk about. But I really must go. That's my cue for me to begin my presentation. You'll excuse me, won't you?"

With that, he left her.

She was shaking with fury as she entered the legendry and quite famous ladies room, which was filled with all the elegance of a bygone era. It boasted floor to ceiling mirrors, a maid to assist with her needs, and pink silk-covered chairs. Long rose print drapes and silken sheers ballooned in the tropical winds through open windows. The lounge had real mahogany doors, which led through the large powder room into a separate area with stalls that were a series of small, separate spaces.

Ordinarily she'd stop and enjoy the ambiance, but she was too shaken by Wolfe to pay as much attention to the room's appointments. When she finished, she washed her hands, absently accepted a linen towel from the attendant, and returned to the wedding.

The reception was in full swing. The punch was a favorite Hawaiian concoction that lightened everyone's spirits, which were already super charged. There was also an open bar and champagne fountain. Mellie knew Nikki would have preferred plain punch, but Mark had done the planning, and he did have associates who liked an occasional drink.

Mellie would have loved to get Nikki's take on Wolfe's surprising arrival, but Nikki was having too much fun to interrupt.

TJ turned up the tempo with his music, and everyone was on their feet dancing. If she wasn't mistaken, that was a conga line forming. She pasted a smile on her face, pulled up her imaginary *Big Girl* panties, threw back a shot from the bar, and joined them.

TJ was busy being a wedding singer and she was busy being Maid of Honor. TJ didn't have the opportunity to follow Mellie. The timing was terrible. He was pulled in all directions and could do nothing. His job was to keep the party going. There were still the traditional bouquet toss and garter catching to get through.

Daisy and Gus bent their heads together and discussed the changes they were witnessing in her.

"She's trying too hard," Gus said.

"Working at having fun, I'd say," Daisy agreed.

"Grabbing shots like that isn't like her." Gus looked concerned as Mellie downed still another.

She had kicked off her heels and was definitely partying.

Daisy noticed that even TJ did a double-take.

When it was time to throw the bouquet, Mellie caught it and promptly burst into tears.

When TJ caught the garter and placed it high on Mellie's leg, she ran crying from the room.

"What did you do?" Gus asked.

"I dunno." Poor TJ looked shell shocked. "I said I loved her. That's supposed to be good, right?"

"Usually, yes. Right words, wrong place maybe? That could explain why she raced out of here. Too much going on. And way too many shots. Daisy's got this. You, son, have a wedding to keep moving."

Daisy went after Mellie.

Gus was on her heels.

"What is it, dear?" Daisy asked.

Mellie was crying too hard to answer right away. "TJ loves me," she finally blurted as if that explained it all.

Daisy waited. "And?"

"Wolfe is here."

"Here! Where?"

"Next door giving a speech."

"Okay. This is no way to be seen by anyone. Gus, get the car while I make her goodbyes. We'll join you in a minute."

Gus got Mellie and Daisy home.

Daisy helped Mellie out of her clothes and into bed. "Things will look better in the morning," she said. "But you'd better take these aspirin to ward off a hang-over."

Mellie took them and crawled into the bed balling into the fetal position.

CHAPTER FOURTEEN: TROUBLED WATER

Mellie

Classes were scheduled to resume on Monday. On Sunday, Mellie skipped the beachside church services she generally liked to attend while Daisy and Gus went off to Mass at St. Augustine's. The church was practically next door.

After Mass, TJ joined them at the condo, bearing her favorite coffee. Fortunately, she was not worse off for the wear, but she was burdened and quiet.

"That's it," TJ announced pulling her body onto his lap.

She was wearing an oversized shirt. "Tell me what is going on. Girls usually don't cry when they catch the bouquet and their lover says the magic L word."

That brought a wan smile to her face." What L word?"

"This one—*love*, as in *I love you*."

Mellie smiled but didn't return the words.

"What's wrong?"

"Dr. Wunderlik is Wolfe."

"Yeah. I know. You introduced us, remember?"

She twisted her hands. "No, he's *my* Wolfe. Well," she amended, "not mine anymore."

"As in your ex, the wolf man?" TJ asked.

"The very same."

"You dumped his ass."

"Yes, but . . ." She drew in a deep breath. "He's filling in for Dr. Rolland until the term ends. I'm in his class."

"He can't do anything. You'll have him on sexual harassment."

Mellie felt terrible.

"We need to think, but even more than that, we need to get out of here and away from the fray." He pulled her by the hand from the room. "I've got just the thing for what ails ya."

In minutes, they were on their way to Kalaheo Beach and windsurfing. Mellie could handle her own board now. She lost herself to the joys of gliding over the sea with TJ at her side and the wind in her hair, but lingering worry and fear in her heart. A sudden swell kept her busy and soon Wolfe and all his drama was left behind like the wave beneath her. She headed out, soaring free across the sea where she wanted to be. As she flew over that beautiful hue of blue known only in Hawaii, healing set in and began taking root.

Later that night, at *The Hat Check Lounge*, she sang Patsy Cline's song, *Crazy*. She sang her heart out. Right now, that song reflected how she felt about Wolfe and their situation. It was making her cray-cray.

She finished and was about to sign off for the evening when out of the corner of her eye she saw a tall man stand to give her a rousing ovation. That man was Wolfe.

The house was on its feet.

She bowed, made her exit, and left the stage.

TJ took over and began his second set.

Wolfe corralled her. "Sit down. Let's talk this out like grownups."

"I may be young, but I'm no child. You can't simply sweet talk me back. We're through. I told you that." She didn't want to cause a scene, so she sat and crossed her arms.

Wolfe leaned across the table. "But, my dear, we *aren't* through. We have unfinished business."

"No. We. Don't."

"You had your temper tantrum, now let's get serious," he said. "You pulled this stunt and got my attention."

"You have some nerve." She worked hard to calm her fury. She knew she could not protest too much. That would indicate she still cared. "I thought I made myself clear. We have no business left to finish."

"Oh, but, my love, we do. You left Michigan so suddenly that I was forced to give you an incomplete. I'll see you tomorrow after class in Dr. Rolland's office. He's kindly letting me use it while I'm here and he's away. You'll either talk to me here or see me in my office."

"I'll see you in hell first." Mellie got up and left work early.

She texted TJ to tell him she was worn out and not to come over.

He didn't.

Mellie spent a restless night stewing. Sleep eluded her, and her stomach churned with anxiety. It unnerved her to see Wolfe again. Part of her, she had to admit, was thrilled that he had come after her. Just as she finally had herself convinced that he was history, he turned up like a bad penny, reminding her that remnants of their relationship were still there. Enough to suck her back in if she wasn't careful . . . very careful.

There was a certain amount of satisfaction knowing that he still wanted her. Although it was upsetting and unsettling, it was strangely flattering, a salve to her bruised heart. Maybe she meant something to him after all?

Aargh! She knew she was vulnerable. No one wanted to be dumped. Unrequited love sucked. Feeling slighted, wronged, rejected, and worse, replaced, sucked, too. She wished she knew what to do.

TJ wanted to punch something. No, someone. He wanted to punch Wolfe. Wisely, he refrained. He needed to see Mellie, needed to tell her that everything was okay, that Wolfe couldn't hurt her anymore. She was with him and that was all that mattered. But the reality was that their love was new and recently shared, and she had not said the words in return.

While windsurfing Mellie had perked up some, but he could tell it hadn't fixed her underlying turmoil. Mellie had class to attend that day, so he decided to pick up her favorite skinny chocolate latte and see her before she left home.

* * *

Mellie was brooding on the lanai, lost in her tortuous conundrum.

Daisy opened the slider-door. "Penny for your thoughts."

"They're not worth that much."

"Wolfe?"

"Yup."

There was a knock at the door. Daisy left to answer it returned with and led TJ, carrying a latte. The ever-rolling sea with its lace topped crests soothed and relaxed her. The graceful palms beside her danced in the trade winds, easing her tension.

"Don't be a wuss, Mellie, stand up for yourself." Daisy dropped her bomb and left them alone.

Mellie had to smile at Daisy's use of the word. Usually, Daisy was such a lady, being so blunt was out of character for her.

Overhearing Daisy's comment apparently surprised TJ, as well. He almost dropped the latte he was carrying as he joined them.

Mellie accepted the latte gratefully, and TJ pulled her onto his lap and kissed her lips, then ran a few more kisses down the column of her neck. Shivers crossed her skin as he made his way to her collarbone.

He hit a spot that made her giggle, and she gently shoved him back from her neck. "I don't know what to do or how to handle Wolfe today. I've been called to his office, and I feel like a kid going to the principal."

"Maintain your distance. Call him Dr. Wunderlik," he advised. "Keep it professional like we do every day. Like our *on land, on sea* policy."

Mellie chewed her lip, trying to fight her doubt. "It's not going to be that easy. He knows all my weak spots. He's my prof and will grade me."

"Your work is thorough. You're done with mid-terms. The grades are posted. You did well, I checked. He can't get you there."

"He'll come up with something. He gave me an incomplete because I left his other class early. He knew my lab notes were finished, but that didn't stop him. I tried to beat him at his own game and transferred to UH, but here he is, in charge of me again." She sighed and slumped in her chair.

"That asshole."

Mellie sipped her latte. "Mm. This is so good. My fav."

"I know. I thought it would help." TJ smiled at her.

"It is. But . . ."

"But?"

"I have to deal with him today." Mellie was firm.

"Being forewarned is being forearmed. We'll beat him. Together. I promise."

Mellie straightened up, threw her shoulders back, and jabbed a finger into his chest. "You can't do anything. This is *my* battle. *My* life. *My* business. *I'm* the one who has to handle it. On my own."

"Who says?"

"*I* say."

TJ pressed his point. "I'm in this relationship too — for the long haul. You don't have to do this alone. Hell, you don't even have to *see* him. You could cut class and still pass, I bet."

"I don't cut classes. That's not the answer."

"I'm just saying."

Mellie glared at him and said in a warning tone, "Look, if you make me talk about this anymore, I'm going to talk about my feelings."

"Aren't we doing that now?"

"Not even barely. If you don't stop insisting, you'll handle this for me, I'll make you talk about *your* feelings and then we'll have a fight."

"Fine. Have it your way," TJ said caving. "Anything but talk about my feelings. Does wanting to punch him out count?"

She laughed. "Very funny. Very mature."

TJ's expression turned serious. "Just where do I stand?"

Mellie's aggravation was growing. "Why are we talking about us suddenly? You said you weren't into commitment, remember?"

"I was a commitment-phobe. I'm not now. Especially with Wolfe man sniffing around you like a dog . . ."

Mellie held up her hand up to stop his words.

"Ok. Try this on." TJ stood, tipping her off his lap, shoulders rigid. "Are you just using me to get back at him, or worse, to get back *with* him?"

Standing herself now, Mellie snapped, "That remark is so insulting that I will not dignify it with a response."

"Too late. You just did."

"TJ, you are seriously ticking me off. You are so close to my last nerve that I might just punch you."

"Your nerves. What about me? You didn't answer my question. Are you secretly hoping to get back with him?"

"Getting to know each other, work, research, Snipe hunting . . ." She ticked each thing off on her fingers. "After all we have done together, how can you even ask that?"

"Just let me be there beside you. Moral support and all," TJ pleaded.

"I'm a big girl. With a brain in her head. Not someone for you to rescue."

"I asked a simple question."

"Which I told you I wouldn't dignify with an answer."

"Fine."

"Fine. Them's fighting words. This is *my* battle, *my* unfinished business, *my* course credit. *I'll* handle it, thank you very much." She strode off, grabbed her book bag, nodded to Daisy, and left TJ in her dust.

CHAPTER FIFTEEN: THE HEART WANTS WHAT IT WANTS

If possible, Mellie was even more miserable than ever. *Men are just idiots.* She wondered if it was a genetic thing. *Are they just wired stupid?*

Wolfe was in rare and true form during the lecture that morning. He showed videos that featured Mellie, reminding her of their research days together. Days that had been happy, fulfilling, and good. Days that had made her feel special, as if she were his protégée and he a supportive mentor. Events they had shared that reminded her of all she had loved about him, and how she had felt when she considered herself his.

Wolfe knew Mellie well and played his hand to his advantage. Mellie was shaken by her memories, the lure of what once was. It was powerful. As she realized Wolfe intended it to be.

After two hours of classwork, Wolfe announced, "Class dismissed."

Mellie gathered her things prepared to leave.

"Miss Wheaton?" he called.

She approached him as he was disengaging his thumb drive from the Smart desk. She could barely lift her gaze to him. She tried to act normal. *Breathe. Just breathe. He doesn't know what's up with you. He can't read your mind. Can't read me like a book. He's not magic.*

"Walk with me." He headed out without looking back, expecting that she would just blindly obey.

She deliberately stayed where she was. She did that sometimes. She did something he wouldn't expect, trying to prove to herself that he didn't have command over her. Couldn't control her after all. She didn't have to succumb to whatever it was that held her enthralled. She wasn't at his beck and call, even though prior programming, grooming, and careful conditioning urged her to comply.

He turned back when he noticed she was not following him. "Really?" he asked. "You want to hash this all out here? In public? With another class coming in?"

Uh. that would be a no. Finally joining him, she gathered herself together and entered Dr. Rolland's office, leaving the door partially ajar. The air in the room felt too close. Or was it just her feelings closing in on her? The images and memories he aroused clouded her mind, but she knew the real him. The heartless man who cruelly slept with her rival. The man she herself had placed on a pedestal. He couldn't do anything to her that she didn't allow.

There was a cozy set-up in the office with two comfortable chairs arranged for conversation. He gestured to them not to the seat across from the desk. He meant to have a more personal contact.

She didn't like this. It'd be harder to be professional if he made this like a confessional. Even a confessional allowed for distance. There was no distance here. She felt like cornered prey.

He reached out a well-manicured hand and touched hers. A frisson of feeling flooded her. She withdrew her hand as if it had been burned.

"Just get to the point," she snapped. "Tell me what you want."

"That ought to be crystal clear. Do I have to spell it out?"

She flushed but pushed on. "To be clearer, what is the issue?"

"There are several." He let that sink in as his gaze probed hers.

She really wanted to cry. *Let this just be over. Why can't this be simple?*

"Here's the trouble, *Shellie Mellie*." He used to call her that. *Do not fall for this bull.*

"There's trouble with a credit. Seems like you aren't a senior ready to graduate yet. You never turned in your last assignment. Perhaps we can work this little issue out before it messes with your graduation and the position it seems that is waiting for you at HMBI."

"What? How do you know about that job?" she asked.

"I make it my business to keep my eye on you. You know that. I always have, I always will. Rolland and I go way back.

"This is a power play." Mellie ground out." What you mean is you'll sign off on that credit when I come back. Don't play me here."

"Damn it. This is no power play. This is the only way I can even get you alone to try to talk some sense into you. Give me a second chance. You know how I feel about you."

"No. There's *a credit* missing. Tell me what to do and I'll do it. This is business, nothing more. I'm really done, Wolfe, with this." She made a gesture between them. "There's no you and me anymore."

"There's more in the field and in life that I can teach you." Wolfe leaned closer to her.

A speculative glint flickered in his eyes for a moment, then it disappeared as if it had never been there. But it was enough. She'd gotten to him and he didn't like it one little bit. She held her ground. She'd win this war.

"I want things that you can't give," Mellie stated once and for all.

"Like what?"

"How about fidelity. That's a biggie you failed to give. True love is another."

"I can do that. I can be good for you."

"No, you can't. You're missing a gene or something. I want marriage someday."

His eyes gleamed. "Okay."

"Yeah, right."

"I do."

"Children."

Wolfe had the good grace to look away.

"See? I told you so. If you loved me for who I am and what I want, these things wouldn't be deal breakers."

Then he kissed her. This is the real deal breaker."

"If you proceed along these lines, *Dr. Wunderlik,* there could be problems for you."

"But you won't pursue that will you?" he said with an air of confidence.

Mellie stood to leave. "This isn't over."

"You've got that right, my *Shellie Mellie.*"

"Don't call me that. I'm not your anything."

"Oh, but you are." To prove it, he kissed her again with barely restrained passion.

For a moment — in that moment only — a torrent of emotion rushed through her. Badly shaken, she raised a finger to her lips, which had felt the full force behind that kiss.

Unfortunately, Dr. Rolland and TJ chose that moment to enter Dr. Rolland's. *Oh, my God. Did they see what happened?*

Furious and upset with herself and everyone else, Mellie grabbed her things. She could only hope Dr. Rolland was not fooled by Wolfe's remarks. She respected Dr. Rolland and didn't want to disappoint him, especially after he had told her she had been highly recommended by the University of Michigan and had come to his attention solely due to the quality of her work.

"Ahem. What on earth is going on here?" Dr. Rolland asked Wolfe.

"Students get carried away sometimes when there's a celebrity of sorts that cause some to cross the lines like she just did. I'm sure she meant nothing by her unfortunate display of affection. Some young women don't take rejection easily."

Mellie felt faint. A stillness stole through her. She was shaking her head vehemently.

"I have my answer," TJ said. "It looks like you have the situation under control, Mellie." Sarcasm laced his voice. "I see why you didn't need my help with this. Looks like I was right."

She froze. *I'm going to be sick.*

Dr. Rolland and TJ consulted with each other in quiet tones.

Wolfe gathered his things, hemming and hawing. "Unwanted, unsolicited attention is an occupational hazard in this profession. She's just forward. I was going to explain things to her . . . Coeds think sex will get them anything they want." He pushed past Dr. Rolland and left.

Mellie rushed out before anyone could say another word.

"That looked like sexual harassment to me," TJ grumbled. "Mellie is no groupie."

"I think so too," Dr. Rolland agreed. "I'll deal with it. He won't get away with it. Right now, TJ, I need you to accompany me with this next leg of my research. Are you good to go? Our flight leaves at 3:45. There's a hurricane advisory out, but the airport is still open. I think we can avoid it."

"Roger that," TJ returned. "I'll be there."

He tried calling Mellie, but it went straight to voice mail. He left a brief professional message, assigning her to another crew. Then he went in search of Gus. He seemed to have become the *go-to* guy for the family.

When TJ got to the condo, Daisy told him Gus was heading off to meet Mark to fill him in on Wolfe's arrival, and to talk about the hurricanes possibly headed their way.

Then Daisy gave him a look he felt down to his soul and shook her head.

"Mercy, but there's a lot going on," she said. "I'll tell you what I told Mark and Nikki, and Caren and Chance for that matter. Life is too short for nonsense. Whatever it is, straighten it out. Don't go by feelings alone. Find the facts."

"That's well and good, but what if the facts are Mellie wants Wolfe?"

Daisy cocked a brow. "You really think so? Has she said as much? I heard an *if* in there. You're not sure what's really happening, are you?"

"No. But she agreed to meet him this morning. Alone. In his office."

"Isn't that how advising meetings usually go?"

"Yes. But when Dr. Rolland and I got there, Mellie was kissing Wolfe."

"Was she now? That doesn't sound like Mellie. Have you asked her about it?"

TJ sighed heavily. "She went off in a huff."

"Doesn't sound like that was good for either you or Wolfe. Gus is meeting with Mark at the Moana. You might bounce this off him, but I think Mellie knows what she doesn't want in her life. Wolfe."

"She told you that?" TJ questioned.

Daisy shook her head. "Not in so many words, but I know her."

"I'm going off to The Big Island with Dr. Rolland and most of my crew. I came here to tell someone, since she's not taking my calls. Fill her in for me?"

"Will do. Think about what I've said. Remember, feelings aren't facts."

TJ got lucky and found Gus as soon as he entered the spacious lobby of the Moana. He approached him and asked for a few moments of his time.

Gus waved him over to a grouping of chairs out of the mainstream. "Trouble in paradise, I'd guess, based on last night alone."

"Way worse than that." TJ complained. "Doctor Rolland and I found Wolfe and Mellie locked in a very close encounter. They were *kissing*."

He explained the whole Wolfe-Mellie encounter, including Mellie running out of the room.

"The heart wants what the heart wants," Gus said. "But in this case, that kiss might have been the test she needed to clear him out of her system. Or she might have had little to do with it. I've been known to steal a kiss myself. Haven't you?"

TJ cringed. He had shamelessly stolen their very first kiss, barely getting consent.

Gus pressed his advantage. "How do you know that didn't happen?"

"It looked like more than that."

"Might have been a *kiss off*, you know, a goodbye."

"Who does that?"

"Appearances are deceiving."

TJ laughed. "As if I don't know that."

Gus looked at him closely. "How so?"

"Mellie thought I was a shiftless surfer dude."

"And I bet you thought she was just some hot chick, didn't you? Without a brain in her little blonde head? All looks and no substance?"

TJ laughed, admitting the truth to that.

"Here's my advice—talk to her. Seems like your heart wants Mellie. Make sure she knows that. And, TJ, while you're at it, give her a chance to listen to hers. She's probably very confused. Two studs after her and all."

TJ stood and shook Gus's hand. "I don't know. That looked like a hot and heavy kiss. I will try to talk to her as soon as I get back from my research on the Big Island. I'm off to the airport. All I know for sure is my heart is hers. For all time. Every time. Not that she wants it."

"All she wanted was to take charge of her own life. You can't fight her battles. Truthfully, is that the kind of woman you want? Male chivalry died out several centuries ago. Today's women want more than tokens of respect. Remember that. When you're ready to take that step, tell her. Until then, go big or go home."

"Thanks, Gus."

TJ headed for the airport, a wreck and confused. He was beginning to wish he had never embarked on this research journey. He wanted to see Mellie. He wanted this to end. He wanted to force her to choose. *Wolfe or me? What's it gonna be? Gus said give her time to hear her heart talk. Can I do that?*

After Mellie left Dr. Rolland's office, she was awash with so much turmoil she didn't know what to do. She was furious with everyone—even herself. *I should have seen that coming. Fool. What did I think would happen? I shoulda known better.*

She found herself driving faster than the speed limit and made a deliberate effort to slow down. She was on her way to meet Nikki for lunch, although what she expected from Nikki she didn't know.

She knew Nikki could not fix this. Only she knew what she wanted. But did she know, beyond a doubt, that she did not want Wolfe?

She did know this much. He had revealed his true character. *Douche bag. What an asshole. And TJ? Was he much better? Treating me like a possession. Wanting to take over. Wanting to fix things for me. Probably pound Wolfe into the pavement. Just because I love him doesn't give him the right to . . . Wait a minute. Love him? OMG. I love him! Now what?*

Nikki was sitting in a wicker chair on the Veranda at the *Moana*. The palm trees were lashing in the strengthening winds. A waiter closed the white sun umbrella over her head and removed it with an apology.

"Sorry. Storm coming in," he said.

Nikki was munching on a spear of succulent pineapple when she saw Mellie and waved her over. The napkin had to be secured under her iced tea, since the winds were increasing. She offered a spear to Mellie.

"No thanks. Be careful. That stuff is lethal."

"This wind is kicking up. A tropical hurricane is threatening. Mark and Gus are at Costco getting water, more food, and supplies in case we have to ride this out." She gestured to the help, who were busy placing sandbags along the outer wall of the Moana while others fastened the shutters into place. "We're going to go back to the condo until further notice. It's set back a bit more than the Moana." Nikki broke off to note, "You look terrible. Too much wedding party?"

"Too much Wolfe."

Nikki raised a brow. "What do you mean? He's history."

Mellie's misery started welling in her eyes. "No, he's here."

"Here? In Hawaii? How?"

"He's here for a conference. He was the keynote speaker. Right here. Last night."

"Back up," Nikki said." I'm confused."

"The conference was held last night in the Banquet Room right next to your reception."

"Good God. No wonder you look like you had no sleep. Tell Mama all about it."

So Mellie did. In detail.

"I can't resist asking." Nikki said and winked. "How was the kiss?"

"After what I've told you, all you want to know about the kiss?" Mellie asked in disbelief. "A hurricane threatens, and you want details of a kiss?"

"Yup. He roars through you like a hurricane so, fess up. It's a fair and relevant question."

Mellie leaned forward. "Toe curling."

Nikki leaned in, too. "So, what did that tell you?"

"He's a good kisser?"

Nikki sat back in her chair as the trade winds increased tossing her hair into her face. "What else?"

"I like his kisses?"

"Mellie . . ." Nikki giggled, then chagrin set in.

"He's characterless. He is not for me. I want better than that. I want a lot more than what he is."

"Good. Now turn around and tell him that." Nikki rose and addressed the man standing behind Mellie. "Wolfe, I presume? I so want to tell you to go screw yourself, but I don't need to. Mellie will tell you herself what a failure of a man you are."

Nikki left Mellie to face Wolfe, hoping she was right about what her sister-in-law would say.

Mellie shook with anger. "You're stalking me?"

"It looks that way. Hear me out here, believe it or not, I get it. "

"Finally."

"I was a fool to cheat on you. I do not deserve you. I would probably cheat again. But Monique has nothing to do with you. It's me. I need to be a better man. I am genuinely sorry. Please forgive me. Let me show you my better side."

Mellie pierced him with a glare.

He flinched.

"Yeah, right. If and when that ever happens, do *not* call me." Mellie stared at him calmly for a moment. "I accept your apology. I just want to be treated with the respect a student like me deserves."

"I know, and I hope when" — he paused, took a breath — "the investigation into our little fiasco occurs, that you would be so kind as to go easy on me."

"Oh, trust me," she said in a succinct tone, "I will tell them everything easily."

"We'll get through these two weeks and you'll never hear from me again, if that's what you really want." Wolfe flashed a smile that appeared filled with regret. "But try to keep this open. You can't know the future. Get TJ out of your system. Sow your oats. I'll be waiting. It's up to you."

CHAPTER SIXTEEN: BATTEN THE HATCHES

Mark cuddled up with Nikki in the condo, watching the weather forecast of Keilani Keo on KITV. The map of the Hawaiian Islands was behind the forecaster as she pointed out the developing storm.

"This just in. Tropical Depression Iselle has been upgraded to *Hurricane Iselle*. Residents are asked to take precautions. Secure all outdoor furniture. Return boats to their slips. Surfers are asked to stay out of the water. All beaches are closed, and the lifeguards have been recalled.

"Tourists are asked to check with the front desk of their hotels. Should evacuation become necessary, all lanes of traffic on Highway H1 will go in one direction. Seek high ground. Check with the airport. Some flights have already been cancelled as *Iselle* gains strength. This is KITV, Honolulu's number one network. We get the job done first. Stay tuned for more weather news. Elsewhere on the island . . ."

"Did you hear that, Nik?" Mark asked. "Good thing we aren't planning to island hop until next week."

"Fortunate for us. How 'bout that?" Nikki said. "I feel like the storm should be named after Mellie. She's all churned up over Wolfe and very upset with TJ. She's whirling with emotion."

"That girl, I do so not want to meet up with her when she's like this. She's bad enough when things are normal."

"Afraid of her roar?"

"Something like that, and a whole host of other things." He leaned in to kiss her. "I'm not in the market for missing any nookie, my lady Don't want to be in the sucked into the drama, don't want to be in the crossfire."

Mellie had received a text from TJ telling her she would crew with another team while he was away, but the weather had closed the campus and schools and a whole host of businesses. Everyone was in *hunker down* mode. She doubted anyone would throw hurricane parties like the newscasters reported happening in Louisiana. No parties were happening around her, at any rate, although she wouldn't mind the rum and fruit juice drink called a Hurricane right about now.

TJ and his regular research crew, along with others of Dr. Rolland's, flew Hawaiian Air to the Big Island with no problems. But they were getting worried about not just one but two storms approaching the islands. The islands had not had a hurricane in twenty-two years, and now two were headed their way. All flights had been cancelled, and no more were expected now that theirs had landed. The airports were open, but no one was going anywhere. All around them people were preparing for the storm. Some team members, himself included, were tracking the warnings on their phones and tablets. He hoped the storms would skip the islands this time.

He was concerned not only about the weather, but also about how Mellie was doing. He still hadn't heard from her.

Dr. Rolland had arranged the use of several small watercrafts to conduct research on the ocean temperatures before, during, and after hurricane activity. The team went out and dropped specimen floats to collect ocean water for analysis, took some reading and samples, and left others to collect afterwards.

Ocean currents could vary and affect the shark population, as could temperature changes in the ocean. Neither TJ nor anyone else was overly concerned about the weather. Hurricanes happened in the tropics, but most storms never hit shore in Hawaii. When they did, there was hell to pay. They were in uncharted waters as never before. Now, back-to-back hurricanes were en route to the Hawaiian chain, and no one knew what to expect.

Noticeable exceptions hit Kauai. The general consensus concerning Oahu was that the mountain ranges changed the weather and the hurricanes broke up before reaching the island. Wind was only part of the problem. The worst damage came from flooding and the storm surge that followed.

The rest of the research team got off the ocean and sought shelter as the surf became higher and rougher. But TJ had noticed a key line that was not well anchored.

"Don't fuckin' do this," Burt pleaded.

But TJ dropped Burt off and returned to the open water alone.

Mellie was extremely upset that she and TJ parted as they did. He was now in harm's way and had no clue that she loved him. She had sent him into the storm without her love and support. He thought she wanted Wolfe, that she had welcomed Wolfe's kiss. The simple truth was she wanted TJ. From the first kiss so early in their relationship, she knew she wanted TJ. She should have welcomed his support.

He simply wanted to protect her from a known danger. He wanted to safeguard her heart. By her own admission, Wolfe wasn't to be trusted. It had taken her a while before she'd realized that TJ wasn't trying to control her or take away her independence. He simply wanted her to be safe from a known predator. Wolfe was no different from the shark that TJ had saved her from that day when she wanted to swim in shark-infested waters. What was she thinking? Now he was in the path of the storm. Mellie's anxiety ratcheted up to an all-time high.

"We interrupt this broadcast with an update on our weather. Hurricane *Iselle* is estimated to hit Honolulu after sunset tonight. Hurricane Julio is on her heels, on track to hit Hilo on the Big Island. Viewers are urged to stay off the streets and to stock up on water and food.

"We've been told that folks have stripped the shelves of Spam and Vienna sausages. Buy anything you can by way of provisions. Shelters have been set up at all local high schools on Oahu and the Big Island. Bring sleeping bags if you have them. Expect to share resources. Pets are welcome. The police are out encouraging the homeless to go to the shelters, as roadways and underpasses may become flooded. Tourists should follow the recommendations of the hotels they are staying in. This is Keilani Keo of KITV reporting."

Mellie and Daisy were glued to the televisions in the condo, watching for storm updates. Daisy kept her attention on CNN on a bedroom TV while Mellie kept tabs on the Weather Channel in the living room. They'd update each other frequently.

"Did you hear that?" could often be heard throughout the condo.

Mellie wrung her hands. Her stomach was a mess. She was already in a turmoil about Wolfe. Add in not one but two hurricanes, and she was a mess. Then there was TJ. Her heart hurt with worry.

Everyone in the family was on edge. Nerves were frazzled.

Even Daisy wasn't nearly as calm as her tone implied. Mark and Gus had yet to return from their shopping trip. The TV reports stated supplies were literally flying off the shelves everywhere, and that they had already run out of bottled water. There was also a run on batteries and flashlights, as everyone was sure the power would go out.

Mellie paced. Her hands twisted, displaying her anxiety. "Daisy! Another storm is heading directly to the Big Island! Most likely TJ's out there collecting ocean samples and temperature readings. He's in the swamp, up to his ass in alligators. He's probably in the direct path of the hurricane, and it's all my fault."

"It is not. If anything, he's surrounded by sharks, just the way he loves it. But no doubt he's hunkered in like the rest of us. He's no fool. That's a smart young man who wants to come home to you."

Mellie shook her head. "Not so much. I told him off but good."

"You think words will bother him? Honey, he's male. He probably only heard half of what you said. He'll be back. Mark my words."

Gus walked in, carrying cases of bottled water. He'd obviously heard what Daisy had said. "That boy's in love, Mellie."

Gus and Mark made several trips lugging supplies, and Mellie and Daisy helped bring them inside. The guys hadn't had any luck finding flashlights, but Daisy had found candles and matches, so they were set to go.

Mark had his battery-operated weather radio set up and ready.

Mellie and Daisy had already secured the lanai furniture by bringing it inside. They'd also closed the shutters over the lanai sliding door. The shutters might look merely decorative, but they were fully functional when needed. They closed the window blinds to afford them as much protection as possible.

Outside, the wind howled. The noises from the roiling surf and wind was deafening.

Daisy left the bedroom, muted the TV, and sat down next to Mellie on the ottoman.

Mellie was happy for her reassuring presence.

Daisy grabbed her hands and looked her straight in the eye. "Fretting about what could be is almost as futile as fretting about this storm. *Que sera sera.* Have faith. It'll be okay. Right here, right now, we are safe. All of us."

Then the power went out.

Dr. Rolland's team took shelter with the others at the local high school. While the hurricane had yet to hit land, the wind, surf, and rain lashed the island with what felt like hurricane force although the winds were under fifty miles an hour.

Burt joined the group and told them TJ had refused to come in. He gave Dr. Rolland TJ's coordinates. Dr. Rolland immediately relayed the coordinates, notifying the coast guard using a ship-to-shore radio frequency.

Mark had turned on his weather radio to follow the hurricane's progress. When he heard a report about TJ, he quickly turned down the volume so Mellie couldn't hear that TJ was lost at sea. But he wasn't fast enough.

All the blood seemed to drain from Mellie's face and she went white. She looked on the verge of fainting.

Mark pushed her head between her knees while Daisy encouraged her to breathe.

"The Coast Guard is out there," Daisy assured her. "FEMA has back up plans for search and rescue. Rescuer swimmers have been on call. He's all right. He's strong."

"He's as dumb as a doorknob. Stupid is more like it." Mark

was beside himself. They were facing a hurricane only to find out that fool was lost at sea somewhere off the Big Island.

TJ struggled to get his small craft back to shore, and one thought drove him more than any other — Mellie. He was not about to lose her and all they had over his ego and stupidity. He prayed he got the chance to see her again, that this hurricane — and the one in his life — would blow over.

A huge swell capsized his boat, and by time he broke the surface, all he could find was an oar. He grabbed hold of it and continued his struggle to get to the shore.

TJ was fighting for his life. He was glad he'd always insisted on safety and had worn his life jacket. The surf was twenty feet high. Just as he came down from one wave, another huge swell would catch him and threaten to drown him.

CHAPTER SEVENTEEN: HANG ON, SLOOPY

Oahu took a pounding but didn't get the hurricane. *Iselle* blew herself out once she hit land, but not before scaring everyone silly and leaving them with downed trees and power lines. Some flooding occurred, but it didn't affect the family. It did slow the flow of goods and services. Businesses and shops remained closed. Clean up crews were busy. But TJ was still out there.

All TJ could think of was Mellie. He clung to his thoughts of her as if she were a life ring. He had to survive these swells, even if they seemed to go on forever. He was caught in the riptide, so he clung to the oar, flowing with the current.

He prayed he'd get the chance to set things straight with Mellie, but the sea was pounding him, and he was tiring. *Is this it? Am I going to die out here?* He could hear nothing but the roar of the sea. He struggled to keep his head above water, to breathe. His kept his thoughts on Mellie. If this was it, then Mellie was his lifeline and last hope.

The current pulled him under, but he still hung onto the oar.

TJ was going under again when, from out of nowhere, help in the form of a coast guard rescue diver swam up behind him. The guardsman attached a clip to a harness he had fastened around each of them, tugged on the coil, and they were lifted to the safety of a helicopter.

"Thanks, man," TJ croaked. "Another minute or so and I'd be fish food. Couldn't hang on any longer."

"You're not supposed to be out in water like this. You were one lucky son of a gun."

"I'm fine. Just get me home to Mellie."

They took him to the hospital, where they kept him under observation for twenty-four hours.

When he woke the next morning, his thoughts returned to Mellie. He prayed she was safe. He ought to have given her more credit. She had got herself this far. In the past, she had stood up to Wolfe on her own in Michigan, and she had proven that she could do so now. He was wrong to think she had initiated any contact with Wolfe. He knew her better than that.

Wolfe had obviously pressed his advantage, tried to keep her off balance. But TJ knew within the depths of his heart that she had not encouraged Wolfe. *That is so over.*

He could see that clearly now. Why couldn't he have just trusted her to do what she had to do herself? *Because you're an idiot.* She was through with Wolfe. He knew that intellectually, but then his stubborn pride and temper had overridden his good sense.

This was not about him or Wolfe. It was all about Mellie. Her life. Her terms. She was an independent woman and didn't *need* either of them. *What a mess.* There was nothing he could do from here, but when he got back, he was going to offer her one huge and humble apology.

TJ had one message to deliver once he saw Mellie again. He'd beg her if necessary. He wanted her to give him a second chance. He'd keep every promise he'd ever made to her and then he'd make a whole host of new ones. He had to get to her as soon as he could to tell her. Her life was hers, but he wanted to share it. On her terms. He'd been stupid to ask her to make a choice, him or Wolfe. *That was fuckin nuts. What was I thinking?*

TJ spent several days on the Big Island before he was able to get a flight back to Oahu and Mellie. The Island had lost power, and palm trees were uprooted, making the roads impassable, but their prayers had worked. Hurricane Julio went north of them. The seas and the winds were rough, the power remained out, and cell phones did not work, as the towers were toppled.

All he could think of was Mellie and how she must be worried. Thank goodness Dr. Rolland had contacts in the Coast Guard and had them notify Mellie that he'd been found safe and sound.

The airports finally opened, and TJ caught the first flight he could back to Oahu. Once there, he headed directly to the condo. Hawaii was back to its perfect weather. The seas were normal, the sky a brilliant blue. He enjoyed the calm as he rode his bike toward his destiny.

Daisy greeted him at the door, and simply said, "You know where to find her."

And he did. He went to *their* beach, where they had picnicked, swam, and windsurfed.

He spotted her immediately, soaring strong across the sea with the wind in her hair. He'd know her anywhere. That golden body. That red Baywatch swimsuit. In a heartbeat, he got his rig ready and caught up with her quickly.

When she saw him, she signaled, and they immediately headed for the shore. Once on the beach, they flew into each other's arms, hearts in their eyes. Not much needed saying. His lips on hers was everything he wanted. He clung to her, murmuring a million apologies, which she readily accepted

"My future is to love you forever." TJ repeated every promise he ever made to her. "I will always trust you to do what's right for you."

Mellie couldn't take her eyes or hands off TJ. She burrowed into the safety of his arms that surrounded her. He held her close to his heart, which was pounding so hard she could feel it. He was home and safe and saying all the right things.

"I trust you to treat me like I have a brain, and that I will use it to take care of myself," she murmured.

"Let's make a deal. I won't push, and you won't run."

"You're on, you stubborn fool. Just because I love you doesn't mean I lost all my senses."

"You do? You love me?" TJ's grin spread almost from ear to ear.

Mellie laughed. She knew she had finally said the words he had wanted . . . needed to hear. "Yes, I do."

"Promise?"

"I do."

"Will you marry me?"

"Say what?"

"Marry me."

Her piercing scream and wild dance gave him the only answer from her heart. *Yes.*

The End

OTHER BOOKS BY KATHY KALMAR

The Beach Series

Beyond the Beach 1
Beyond the Beach 2
Beyond the Beach 3
Beyond the Beach 4
Beyond the Beach 5
Back to the Beach 1 (Book 6 in the Beach Series)
Back to the Beach 2 (Book 7 in the Beach Series)
Promises on the Beach 1 (Book 8 in the Beach Series)

The Mountain Series

Mountain Hot, (Book 1)
Mountain Christmas (Book 2)
Mountain Skye Prequel to the Weather Girls (Book 3) Mountain Joy (Book 4)
Mountain Kiss (Book 5)
Mountain Holly (Book 6)
Mountain Promises (Book 7)
Mountain Silver (Book 8)
Mountain Mistletoe (Book 9)
Mountain Bred, (Book 10)
Mountain Led (Book 11)
Mountain Wed (Book 12)
Mountain Hook–up (Book 13 to be published)

Mountain Due (Book 14 to be published)

eXtasy Books Inc.

YOU MAY ALSO ENJOY THE FOLLOWING FROM EXTASY BOOKS:

Mountain Wed
Kathy Kalmar

Excerpt

It was a glorious fall. The weather was warm with cool nights, which brought out the scarlets, reds, and oranges of the sugar maples. Poplars were crowned with sunny yellow, and brown oak leaves provided a welcome contrast. An undulating, leafy network of hardwood trees echoed the colorful leaves everywhere to fashion an autumn ablaze with splendor and unparalleled beauty.

Fall was a peak season for tourists, and Marsha's favorite season. It provided a bountiful harvest of seeds and petals needed for her stock in trade. When she gathered the fruits of the season, she felt reconnected to Mother Earth, Gaia, as well as her Cherokee roots.

Operating her own apothecary connected her new-age spiritualism with her mountain heritage. It allowed her to spread healing, health, and mountain peace to its people. Her only wish was to find something to bring John peace.

The war had done a number on him. While healthy in body, his soul and mind were tormented in the aftermath of war, destruction, and death. The few times he talked about the nightmares, he told her the carnage plagued his dreams and robbed him of sleep. In a heartbeat, something or someone would trigger him, sending him into a fathomless hell. Anything could set off his descent. Once she'd sliced her finger while paring an apple, and John's white, terror-stricken face told her he was reliving something. His strong firm hands shook as he rinsed her finger and examined her thumb. His breath came in huge heaving gulps.

"I'm okay, John. It's fine . . ."

But it was clear John was not okay. He was shaking, and once he bandaged her, he left her alone for hours. Just took off. Like a banshee was after him. She tried to get him to talk about it when he returned, but he shut her out.

"I'm fine. Don't worry."

Marsha used the ground leaves of valerian mixed with cannabis to calm his spirits, and passionflower and chamomile, to ease his nightmares. She added this to any tea she served him from sweet tea to hot varieties. She applied compresses laced with valerian but to no avail. Frequently she burned sage in their bedroom to bring the peace he so needed. Thankfully the negative ions released by the pines and the soothing whispers of breezes through the evergreens helped. Still, sometimes she wished she had the perfect elixir to offer. Most of the time, John appeared to cope and lived his life carving with the other craftsmen, looking forward to the births of his twins. But when the demons roared, he was lost to her and his surroundings.

Marsha pushed her worries away and was often in a contemplative but merry state when John got home from his work at the family owned and operated Lodge. She reveled in her pregnancy and spent her spare time making baby clothes. She also created talcum powders to use for her babies, and other elixirs and teas to help Marion, her mother, as well.

John spent his time working at the Lodge or on the cabin, and Marsha continued making and selling her products from her apothecary. When she wasn't doing that, she spent time applying lotion to her mother's failing body. Trying to bolster it with the latest herbal remedies that Dr. Cyd—as she had begun to call her friend—suggested.

When Marsha broached the topic of a water or home birth, Dr. Cyd stopped her with a simple declarative statement. "You may have twins." Wisely, Marsha did not mention doulas or mountain mid-wives.

It wasn't long before the approach of their first Christmas together as man and wife. Their lovemaking was gentle. At first, he had treated her like she was made of crystal or fine china. As the babies grew, he began to feel more comfortable and became quite inventive as the infants enlarged her body.

He'd chased her around the house with mistletoe, and when he cornered her, he'd often led her to the bedroom. Decorating had become an everyday event until her pregnancy discomfort intruded.

Emma Jean swore she had never seen more mistletoe in her life. "You leave that poor girl alone, John."

Unfortunately, despite the cannabis, Marsha was acutely uncomfortable during the latter stages of her pregnancy. Her ankles had swollen, and morning sickness became morning, noon, and night sickness. "Pregnancy isn't all it's cracked up to be."

Emma Jean and Marion agreed.

"It ends with a bang," her mother counseled.

Marsha tried yoga, hoping the stretching would help ease her discomfort. She and John attended Lamaze training, which again offered no relief.

Emma Jean was beside herself with joy over the impending birth of grandchildren. The pregnancy seemed to help Marion, as well. Marsha laughed when she overheard the two of them discussing becoming memaws.

Marsha knew Emma Jean went through agony waiting and worrying about her son, knowing his internal battle was ongoing. The family often witnessed his shouts and cries, resulting from his horrific experiences in Vietnam. His helicopter had been shot down on the way to pick up some wounded. For a brief time, he and his friend, Charlie, had been held by the Viet Cong. The army had listed them as MIAs, missing in action. That he had served as a medic helped. He had been able to treat many of his buddies, who were also captive and often victims of impaling from bamboo spear booby traps.

One time, John told her about treating a private, a puny, war beaten kid. He said the only things holding the patient together were the bandages he applied. He knew, in his gut, that guy wouldn't make it back to the base, let alone home. John was quiet after that. Marsha put her arms around him to hold him, but he pulled away. With time, she realized he was trying to spare her.

"Let me comfort you, John."

John looked at her. In a grave tone, he said, "Won't do him no good. Ain't no comfort for a thing like this, a man like me."

He often said that the men hadn't been able to tell who was an enemy and who was not. Guerilla warfare had been in play, and the conventional training they had received was often insufficient. Add in the jungle, the heat, the snakes, and the insects, and it had been a literal hell on earth.

Finally, returning home to the Lodge had been John's first step toward real healing. The Lodge seemed to be a magical place made even more so when Marsha came back to it. Thank heaven for the Lodge and his parents.

The Lodge was originally a rustic inn built to house the lumber industry's workforce during its advance into the Great Smoky Mountains. The timber barons had depleted the East Coast timber and moved their operations southward to the Elkmont area. Fortunately, lumbering was a thing of the past now, and a nice hardy second growth of trees covered the once denuded hills once more.

After the lumber industry had logged its last load, Emma Jean's parents had reopened the inn as a lodge for travelers as far away as Georgia and as near as Knoxville.

When Emma Jean and her husband took over, they re-named the inn Sugarlands Lodge after the sugar maple trees growing profusely on the property. They also had expanded, making the delicious maple syrup they provided to the townsfolk. The locals simply dubbed it the Lodge. John helped to run the place when he could tear himself away from whittling and wood crafting. Any spare time John had was spent either in the woods looking for downed hardwoods or spent with Marsha.

She and John frequently visited their cabin as John worked to repair it. He was just adding some finishing touches, so it would be ready to move into soon.

They currently resided at the Annex, a separate section of the Lodge that housed several apartment-like suites. They had their privacy but were still connected to the Lodge.

Marsha spent a lot of her time reviewing the notes she had on pregnancy garnered from her years of study at Berea College and time spent with her grandmother. She also applied what had Cyd taught her, trying special herbs and tea blends to promote wellness. She meditated, burned sage incense, used essential oils and candles, plus played soothing music along with her favorite folk and rock tunes. She talked to her babies and read to them, believing they could hear inside the womb. She ate as healthy as she could, including veggies and fruits, whole grains, and nuts. This was difficult when morning sickness intervened. She had to carry a bucket around for the times she couldn't get to the bathroom in time. That's when she left nuts out of her diet.

The approach of their first Christmas was marked by their first Christmas tree. John made beautiful hand-carved wooden rattles for the babies and a double cedar cradle in which to place the newborns. His skill had grown in the years the army had him. He had told her he whittled away his time whenever he could while in Vietnam. He had sent his carved rosewood pieces home where he knew Emma Jean would display them with pride. Marsha knew he hoped they brought his ma comfort. Though he wasn't there, at least Emma Jean had been surrounded by things he had carved. Marsha was proud of the fact his work was now getting recognized. More than one souvenir shop carried his black bear and deer carvings.

ABOUT THE AUTHOR

Kathy Kalmar, born in Detroit, Michigan, lives with Larry, her husband of nearly four decades. Lately, she feels her life has taken a bad country song turn, since her beloved dog died, her insides were removed, her Smoky Mountain round house burned down in the Chimney Tops II fire in 2016, her computer crashed, and she got scammed by the fired builder. Phew. Her current residence is enlarged by four feet by their new puppy, Valentina. Her new mountain home is —at long last—under construction. She loves to read and write contemporary romance novels. Meanwhile, she remains fond of hot tubbing, chocolate, and sipping wine and mai tais whether at home, Waikiki, or Tennessee. Y'all come back, hear? Currently, she is writing her next book. Aloha and Mahalo.

Contact Kathy at KathyKalmar.com